EXPLOSIVE Adventures

ALEXANDER McCALL SMITH

Illustrated by
Kate Hindley

BLOOMSBURY
LONDON OXFORD NEW YORK NEW DELHI SYDNEY

Bloomsbury Publishing, London, Oxford, New York, New Delhi and Sydney

The Popcorn Pirates first published in Great Britain in 1999
by Scholastic Ltd
The Bubblegum Tree first published in Great Britain in 1996
by Scholastic Ltd

This edition published in September 2015 by Bloomsbury Publishing Plc
50 Bedford Square, London WC1B 3DP

www.bloomsbury.com

Bloomsbury is a registered trademark of Bloomsbury Publishing Plc

A CIP catalogue record for this book is available from the British Library

ISBN 978 1 4088 6586 6

MIX
Paper from
responsible sources
FSC® C020471

Typeset by RefineCatch Limited, Bungay, Suffolk
Printed and bound in Great Britain by CPI Group (UK) Ltd, Croydon CR0 4YY

1 3 5 7 9 10 8 6 4 2

For Wilfred Worsfold and Lana Paun

THE POPCORN PIRATES

~ 1 ~
The Popcorn Islands

Have you ever heard of the Popcorn Islands? Probably not. Very few people have – but if you look hard at a map of the Caribbean Sea, you might just see four little dots not far from Jamaica. The dots won't be named, of course – they're too small for that – but those are the Popcorn Islands.

Not long ago, nobody lived on these islands. From time to time, sailors were shipwrecked on them, and sometimes stayed for months, or even years. Sooner or later, though, they would be rescued and the islands would be deserted again. The shipwrecked sailors were often rather sad to go, as these were comfortable islands, with plenty of fresh water and lots of wild fruit trees. The turtles and birds who lived on the islands were also very friendly, as they hardly ever saw any humans and were always pleased to have some company.

Then, almost one hundred years ago, Lucy's great-grandfather, who was a ship's captain, sailed past the islands and decided to drop anchor and explore them. He liked them a great deal, and his wife, who always went with him on his voyages, liked them even more.

"Let's stay here," she said to her husband, as they sat on the beach and watched the turtles lumbering up from the water's edge. "Let's stay here and build a house. I'm tired of sailing around and never staying in one place very long. I want to have a house, with curtains, and sleep in a real bed, with legs, instead of a hammock."

"I know how you feel, my dear," mused the Captain. "I'd like to look out of my window and see hills, and trees with birds in them, instead of just waves and more waves."

"And eat fresh pumpkins," continued his wife, "instead of dry biscuits and salted ham."

The captain spoke to his sailors, and they all agreed that this was a very good idea. They too had had enough of pulling sails up and down and singing sea shanties as they climbed the rigging. They wanted to have little houses, too, with taps that ran fresh water, and plates that didn't always taste of salt when you licked them. So they left the Captain and his wife and took the ship off and fetched their own wives and children. Then they returned to set up home on the Popcorn Islands. And that is how it all started. It was as simple as that.

As the years went by, the number of people on the islands grew. By the time that Lucy's grandfather was born there were fifty people on each of the four islands, and by the time that Lucy herself arrived, there were one hundred and twenty-five people on each. And that was about right, as it meant that there were just enough people for everybody to be able to find friends, and not so many that the islands became crowded.

It was Lucy's grandfather who made the great discovery that was to give the islands their name. In his day, they had no real name, and were simply called Big Island, Middle Island, Small Island and Tiny Island. Then one day, when he was wondering whether he would plant pumpkins and melons again that year, he made the amazing discovery that the soil of the islands was suitable for growing popcorn. In fact, it was perfect for it. If you put some popcorn under a shallow covering of the islands' rich, dark soil, within a few days a strong little popcorn plant would be pushing its way up into the light.

Then, less than six weeks later, you would have a lush crop of popcorn ripening in the sun, ready to be picked.

It was a marvellous discovery and everybody was quite overjoyed.

"It will be a great change from growing pumpkins," people said. "Imagine having all the popcorn we could possibly want, right here on our doorsteps!"

"And we can sell it too," said another. "We can send it off to America by boat. They love popcorn there!"

"We'll all become rich!" said another. "Fancy that!"

Well, not everybody became rich, but certainly they did very well out of popcorn, and soon there was a thriving trade. From then on, it seemed natural to call the islands the Popcorn Islands. It suited them so well, and the people were proud to come from a place with a name like that.

They were, not at all surprisingly, all very happy — until things suddenly went very badly wrong.

~ 2 ~
The Popcorn Ship Arrives

Lucy lived on one of the popcorn plantations on Big Island. She had a brother, Sam, who was a couple of years younger than she was, and a friend, Hermione, who lived on the neighbouring plantation. She and Hermione spent most of their time together, and even at night they could send messages to one another by torch. All you had to do was to stand at your bedroom window and flash the message out across the darkness of the popcorn fields. Then the answer would come back through the night: *flash, flash, flash!*

During the popcorn-picking season, the island school was closed. This allowed all the children to play their part in bringing in the harvest, which was something everybody had to do. Even the island teacher and the island policeman had to lend a hand. And at the end of it all, when the popcorn crop was safely harvested, everybody had a wonderful party on the beach, with people singing the old popcorn-picking songs and eating as much of everything as they could possibly manage.

There were dancing competitions, too, and Sam always did very well at these. He was double-jointed, which meant that he could dance under a pole which was only a couple of hands' width above the ground. Everybody enjoyed watching Sam show just how bendy his bones were and they clapped and cheered when he finished his performance.

The next day, the popcorn ship was due to arrive. This ship came without fail

the day after the harvest was completed
and everybody would go down to the
harbour to welcome it. Captain Foster,
who owned the ship, was very popular on
the island as he always allowed the children to come aboard and drink the special
lemonade that he made for them. It tasted

like no other lemonade, and everybody was allowed to drink as much of it as they wanted.

Captain Foster had a dog, Biscuit, who was also popular with the children. He was not a very large dog, and he walked in a peculiar way, sideways rather than forwards. Yet he was very friendly, and would bark with delight when any of the children came on board.

Lucy was one of the first to welcome Captain Foster on that particular day. She and Sam ran down to the harbour and were soon joined on board by Hermione. They gave lemon drops to Biscuit, who could not resist them, and chatted to

Captain Foster while they drank their lemonade. Then, when everybody had had enough lemonade, the serious business of loading the popcorn began.

The loading of the popcorn usually took the whole day, and again everybody had to lend a hand. Then, when the last sack had been put into the hold and the hatches lowered into place, everybody went ashore to wave farewell to Captain Foster and Biscuit. The Captain did not like to spend too long in the harbour, as he had a long way to sail with his cargo of popcorn and he knew that he would have to return straight away to get the second half of the crop.

Lucy and Hermione ran down to the beach near the harbour and waved to Captain Foster as the popcorn ship sailed out into the open sea. Then, when it was no more than a dot on the horizon, they went home.

That night, Lucy flashed a message through the darkness. "When do you think Captain Foster will be back?" she asked, in the special code that they had invented.

Flash, *double flash*, *flash*, *flash*, came the reply, which meant, "I think he'll be back next Sunday, although he might make it by Saturday."

Lucy thought that it might be Monday, as she had heard that there were storms at sea and these might hold Captain Foster up. They were both to be proved wrong. The next day, as Lucy was sitting reading in her room, she heard her brother shout from his tree house in the garden.

"The popcorn ship!" yelled Sam. "Look! Captain Foster's back!"

Lucy ran outside to see if her brother was imagining things. But he was not: for there, coming into the harbour, was the unmistakable shape of the popcorn ship. Captain Foster had returned already!

Lucy ran down to the harbour, to find Hermione waiting for her. Then, when the ship had been tied up, she and her friend rushed aboard to find out what was wrong. They found Captain Foster on the front deck, and they could tell immediately that there was something very seriously wrong. Even Biscuit, who normally barked a welcome to the girls, was silent, his head lowered, his tail drooping sadly between his legs.

"We've been robbed," said Captain Foster miserably. "Every last sack has been taken."

Lucy glanced towards the hold. The hatches were wide open, and there was clearly nothing at all inside.

"Who robbed you?" she asked. "How did it happen?"

Captain Foster sighed. "Pirates," he said. "They found me just about four hours off the island and they came aboard. They took everything, even Biscuit's dog food."

Lucy and Hermione gasped. Pirates! They had heard of pirates, of course, as everybody had, but were there still pirates on the prowl, even today? Somehow they seemed to belong to the history books, when people really feared the Jolly Roger flying from the mast. Surely that sort of thing didn't happen any longer?

It was as if Captain Foster could read their thoughts.

"Yes," he said. "I know that everybody thinks that pirates are a thing of the past, but they still exist, believe me! They aren't quite so bad as they used to be, I suppose, but they're still pretty wicked. In the old days they would have made me and Biscuit walk the plank – at least they didn't do that!"

Later, in the kitchen of Lucy's house, over a bowl of soup which Lucy's mother had prepared for him, Captain Foster told everybody what had happened.

"The first I knew of it," he said, "was when I saw a ship in the distance. I didn't think much of it, as there are quite a few ships sailing about out there, but there was something about this one which soon made me take notice. She was sailing straight towards me, you see.

"I thought at first that she might be in trouble. We sailors help one another out, you know, and so I stopped my engine and stayed where I was. In a few minutes they were up alongside me and I saw that she was a large sailing ship, with great white sails and a long pole at the prow. She was a beautiful ship, really, and I suppose that is why I didn't notice at first that there was a black flag fluttering from the foremast.

"They came up beside me and threw a rope across. Then, when they were close enough, a couple of men jumped aboard. I was beginning to worry a little bit now, because these men did not look in the slightest bit friendly, and I could tell that they clearly needed no help from me.

"Biscuit didn't like the look of them either, because he gave a growl and then a loud bark. One of the men looked at him, and then gave him a good kick, sending him shooting across the deck.

" 'Don't you treat my dog like that!' I shouted angrily.

" 'You keep quiet!' said one of the men fiercely, drawing a knife from his belt. 'You just open your hatch for us.'

"I realised that I had no choice but to do what they ordered, and so I opened the hatch and had to stand and watch while they unloaded every single sack of popcorn and tossed it over into their own ship. Then, when they had finished, they got a piece of rope and tied me to the mast. They thought this was very funny, and they laughed as they jumped back on to their own ship and sailed away.

"I was in a spot of bother. As you know, my ship is a single-handed one and there was nobody there to help me. We could drift for days like that, and even run into rocks somewhere. So I more or less gave up any hope of being saved.

"I had forgotten about Biscuit – as had the pirates. No sooner was their ship out of sight than he bounded up to me and started to tug away at the rope with his teeth. It took him some time, but at last he did it, and I was loose. So I turned round and came straight back here to tell you all about it."

"Thank goodness for Biscuit," said Lucy. "Without him . . ."

"Yes," said Captain Foster. "He saved my life."

"But what are we going to do now?" asked Lucy's father. "What are we going to do about the rest of the popcorn? Surely you won't want to set sail with it tomorrow. Those pirates could still be lurking out there somewhere."

Captain Foster thought for a moment. There was clearly a risk that the pirates would return, but he couldn't stay on the island for ever. They had to get the popcorn off to market somehow, and if he didn't take it, then who would?

"I'll have to set sail again tomorrow," he said. "I really don't think there's anything else I can do."

~ 3 ~
Hermione Has An Idea

That night, Lucy lay in her bed and thought about Captain Foster's plight. It would be only too easy for the pirates to raid his ship again, and if that happened there would be no popcorn at all to sell. How would people live, if they couldn't sell any popcorn? Everybody would go hungry and have to live on pumpkins. The thought made her shudder. Pumpkins for breakfast, lunch and supper – for months on end! And pumpkin sandwiches at school as well!

She got out of bed and went to her window. It was completely dark, and even the sea-grape tree outside her window was no more than a large black shape. She looked in the direction of Hermione's house, out across the fields. Would her friend still be awake, she asked herself. Was she also wondering what to do?

Lucy got her torch out of her cupboard and returned to the window. Then, pointing the torch out into the darkness, she flashed her signal.

"Are you still awake?" she asked.

For a few moments nothing happened, and Lucy decided that Hermione must be asleep. But then, through the darkness, a pinpoint of light flashed out.

"Yes. I've been lying here thinking. I'm so worried about Captain Foster and the pirates that I can't go to sleep."

"So am I," replied Lucy. "Surely there's something we could do."

Flash, *flash-flash*, *double flash*, *flash*, *flash*, went Hermione, which meant, "Perhaps we could go with him. We could keep a lookout for the pirates while he sails the ship."

Lucy thought for a moment before she replied. "But what if we see them? What then?"

Hermione's answer came back through the darkness. "If we see them in time, then we'd have a good chance of getting away. Captain Foster's ship is quite fast."

Lucy was not sure about this plan, but it seemed to her that unless anybody came up with a better idea, it was worth trying.

"Let's tell them about it tomorrow morning," she signalled back.

"Yes," flashed Hermione. "Good night."

Lucy went back to bed. Hermione was well known for having good ideas, but Lucy was not so sure about this one. Still, she thought, even a bad plan is better than no plan at all.

The next morning, Hermione arrived at Lucy's house well before the rest of the household was out of bed. She and Lucy discussed their plan, before revealing it at the breakfast table to Captain Foster and Lucy's parents.

"Would it help if you had some warning of the pirates?" Lucy asked the Captain, as he put marmalade on his toast.

"Yes, I'm sure it would," replied Captain Foster. "But when it's just you sailing a ship you don't have time to keep a lookout. And you've also got to stop the ship to get some sleep, you know. And then there's nobody to see what's happening."

Lucy glanced at Hermione, who nodded encouragingly.

"We'll be your lookouts," said Lucy. "Hermione and I have discussed it, and we'd like to come along."

"With me!" said Sam, who had been listening to all this with interest. Nobody had asked him, but he was determined that he would not be left out.

"Oh, I couldn't," said Captain Foster. "It's far too dangerous."

"But we'd be able to get away from the pirates," Lucy said. "You said that they only had a sailing ship. You've got an engine on your ship."

Captain Foster stroked his beard and looked at Lucy's parents, who were whispering quietly to one another.

"We'll let them go," said Lucy's father. "That popcorn simply has to get through. If the children can help, then I think we should let them."

Captain Foster still looked doubtful, but he realised that there really might be no other way, and so eventually he agreed.

Now all that remained to be done was to ask Hermione's parents, and when they heard what was planned, they agreed to let her go.

"Remember your toothbrush, though," said Hermione's mother, who tended to fuss a bit. "And if you do see any pirates, I don't want you to pick up any rough manners from them. Do you understand?"

There was not much time left for preparations. While everybody else helped to load the popcorn on to the ship, the three children packed their bags and made sure that they had everything they needed. Hermione's father spent the whole day making pies for the voyage, and Lucy's mother, who was the quickest sewer on the island, made three splendid sailor suits for the children to wear.

Then, when everything was ready, Lucy, Hermione, and Sam set off for the harbour, wearing their new sailors' outfits and carrying their bags of provisions.

"Welcome aboard!" said Captain Foster from the top of the gangway. Biscuit, who was standing beside him and who was very pleased at the prospect of more company on the voyage, gave a loud bark of delight.

The whole island had turned out to wave them goodbye, and as the ship slipped out of the harbour, the three children stood on the deck and waved and waved until their arms could wave no longer. The people on the shore were smaller now, and soon they were no more than dots.

Lucy looked at Hermione. Her friend was always very brave, and this made her feel brave too, but now, as they faced the open sea, the thought of pirates made her shiver.

"I hope we don't see the pirates," she confessed to her friend. "I'm a little bit scared."

Hermione smiled. "So am I," she whispered back. "But let's try not to show it! We wouldn't want Sam to know."

Sam, who was standing next to Biscuit, turned and whispered into the dog's ear.

"I'm rather frightened, Biscuit," he said under his breath. "But please don't tell the girls."

Biscuit wagged his tail and gave a bark. He wasn't in the slightest bit afraid of pirates, and if they showed their faces around the popcorn ship again, they were going to get a very nasty surprise from him!

~ 4 ~
Unwelcome Visitors

They had set sail in the mid-afternoon and by the time they lost sight of land it was almost sunset. They had had a busy few hours, unpacking their bags and slinging up their hammocks down below, and now Captain Foster was telling them their duties.

"The night is divided into watches," he said. "A watch will be four hours long and you'll have one watch each. You'll start, Sam, because you're the youngest, and then it'll be Lucy and Hermione, one after the other. That'll take us through to morning."

"What do we do?" asked Sam. "Do we steer the ship?"

"No," said Captain Foster. "I'll put down the sea anchor later on and we'll switch off the engine. So all you'll have to do is keep a good lookout for any other ship. If you see anything, come down and wake me up."

"It could be pirates, you see," explained Hermione, making everybody shiver slightly as she mentioned the word.

Sam nodded. If there were going to be pirates, he very much hoped that they would come in somebody else's watch.

They had dinner together, eating two of the pies which Hermione's father had made. It was dark now, and everybody felt lonely and far from home. The sea around them was gentle, with only the smallest of waves, and the sky above was a great dome of stars. You feel bigger on land, thought Lucy. Out here you feel very, very small.

The best place for the watch was right at the front of the ship. Sitting there in the darkness, one would see the lights of any approaching ship and there would be plenty of time to wake Captain Foster. Sam felt very nervous during his watch, but nothing happened while he was up there and eventually the time came for him to go off to wake his sister. He felt very proud of himself, and very pleased that his duties were over.

Lucy took some time to wake up, but eventually she struggled out of her hammock and made her way up on deck. The hours seemed to pass very slowly, but at last she too was finished, and it was Hermione's turn.

Nothing at all happened that night, and the children were beginning to feel a bit more confident by the time that Captain Foster got up and started the engines again. Soon they were ploughing through the sea once more, with a fresh wind behind them helping them on their way, and wonderful-smelling breakfast sizzling away on the cooker.

After breakfast, they again took it in turns to sit up on deck and keep a lookout. Other ships were sighted now, but each time that Captain Foster was called he looked through his telescope and shook his head.

"Banana boat on the way from Barbados," he would say. Or, "Pleasure yacht from Florida, going over to the Caymans."

There was no sign of the pirates, and everybody began to think that the last time they had struck it had just been bad luck. Perhaps that was the last they had heard from them, and the pirates would just be a bad memory.

Then, shortly after lunch, while Sam was keeping lookout, he gave an excited shout.

"Captain!" he called. "A ship off to starboard, coming our way, I think!"

Captain Foster came out of the wheelhouse and put his telescope to his right eye. Lucy and Hermione strained their eyes to see too, but the ship was too far away and it still looked no more than a black smudge on the horizon.

Captain Foster lowered his telescope and frowned.

"I don't like the look of that," he said. "I can't be certain – it's still a bit far away – but I'm going to increase our speed a little and change our course by a few degrees. You keep a very close watch on her, will you?"

He passed the telescope to Lucy and pointed in the direction of the distant ship.

"Let me know the moment she does anything unusual," he said. "I'll be in the wheelhouse."

Lucy took the telescope and trained it on the other ship. She could make out a bit more now, but it was still very far away. As she did so, she heard the note of the ship's engine change slightly as Captain Foster increased speed.

For the next fifteen minutes, the children kept an eye on the distant ship. It seemed to be on the same course as

themselves, they thought, and very slowly it was getting closer. They were now able to make out its masts, and at one point Lucy thought that she could see one or two people on the deck.

"Go and tell Captain Foster that it's following us," Lucy said to Sam.

Sam passed on the message and Captain Foster came up on deck and took the telescope from Lucy. He studied the other ship for a few moments, and then lowered the telescope.

"It's them," he said. "I recognise their ship!"

"Can't we go any faster?" asked Hermione. "Can't we just sail away from them?"

Captain Foster sighed. "I'm going full speed as it is," he said. "But they've got a pretty stiff wind behind them and they're gaining ground."

The children looked at Captain Foster in dismay. Did this mean that the pirates would catch them? And if they did, what then? Would they all be tied to the mast, as the pirates had done to Captain Foster the last time? Or might they even change their minds and make them walk the plank?

Captain Foster saw how worried the children were, and he tried to reassure them.

"We're not beaten yet," he said. "You stay up here. I'm going to go down below and see if I can tinker with the engines to get a bit more speed. Lucy, just take the wheel for me, will you?"

Ten minutes later, Captain Foster came up on deck again. The pirate ship was a bit closer now, and it was possible to make out the rigging on its high masts and see the distant fluttering of its black flag. Captain Foster looked at the approaching ship and herded the children into the wheelhouse. Then he addressed them gravely, as a captain might before his ship goes down.

"It looks as if they're going to catch us," he said. "I have a duty to make sure that you people are not harmed. So what you are going to do is hide, all three of you, and Biscuit too. I don't want him making any trouble with the pirates."

"But what about you?" asked Lucy. "We can't just let you face them alone."

"It will be far better that way," said Captain Foster. "They'll take the popcorn and then they'll probably tie me up, the same as before. But once they've got back on to their ship, you can come out and set me free. It's the best thing to do, as far as I can see."

The children had to agree, although they all felt that they were rather letting Captain Foster down. He showed them to their hiding place, which was at the back of the wheelhouse, under a pile of old popcorn sacks. If they stayed quite still, then none of the pirates would dream of looking in a dusty old pile of sacking. They should be perfectly safe.

"Right," said Captain Foster briskly. "In you get. Stay absolutely quiet and don't make any movements, whatever happens. And if anybody wants to do any sneezing, you'd better do it now!"

Lucy and Hermione fitted under one sack, and Sam and Biscuit under another. Then Captain Foster stood back and checked to see that they were properly hidden.

"Good work," he said. "Now remember what I said about staying still."

The children did not have long to wait. Ten minutes later they heard a shout from above and a jolt ran through the ship.

"They're coming aboard," whispered Hermione. "The pirates are here!"

~ 5 ~
Biscuit's
Mistake

It was difficult trying to keep still under those old popcorn sacks. Lucy's legs were in an uncomfortable position and she would have loved to be able to stretch them, but she couldn't, of course. For Hermione, the worst part about it was not being able to see what was happening. If only she had had a little hole in the sacking to peer through, she would have felt much better. There's nothing worse, she thought, than being hidden and not knowing whether somebody is standing right next to you, or even looking down at you, wondering what those peculiar shapes under the sacking might be.

And as for Sam, he was busy trying to keep Biscuit still. The little dog had started off being quite happy under the sacks, but now he was showing signs of having had enough of this peculiar game and wanting to get out. So Sam had to stroke him and tickle him under his hairy chin to keep him amused.

After some time, the sound of thumping and bumping from the hold came to an end. The sacks must now have been unloaded, and, with any luck, the pirates might sail away.

"Only a few more minutes," Lucy whispered to Hermione. "Then we can get out and —"

She was interrupted by the sound of footsteps. They heard the door of the wheelhouse open and there were voices.

"So where do you keep your money?" asked a rough voice.

"There isn't very much," came Captain Foster's voice. "I keep telling you that. Anyway, it's not here — it's down below. There's nothing in here for you."

"Oh, yes?" came another voice, a cruel, horrible voice that sent shivers down the spine. "You seem very keen to keep us out of the wheelhouse, doesn't he, Bert? So what are you hiding in here?"

"Nothing," said Captain Foster quickly. "Nothing at all."

"We'll be the judge of that," said the first voice. "I think that we might take a little look round, just to be sure. What do you think, Stinger?"

The pirate called Stinger grunted his agreement. "Why not, Bert? You never know your luck. That's what I always say."

Lucy reached out and gripped Hermione's hand. This is the end, she thought – they're bound to find us.

They felt the vibration of footsteps through the planks of the deck. Then they stopped.

"What's in those sacks?" asked Bert.

"Nothing," said Captain Foster, his voice almost breaking with fear. "They're just old popcorn sacks."

Bert snorted. "You should keep your ship tidier," he said. "Just like us."

Then Stinger spoke. "Come on, Bert," he said. "We can't spend all day here. Let's go."

And at that point, Biscuit barked.

You couldn't really blame Biscuit. He had been very good until then, but at last it was just too much for a dog to bear, and he barked. He had recognised the voice of one of the pirates, and he was filled with indignation. How dare these people come back on to his ship? No self-respecting dog would allow them to get away with it.

"Ah!" shouted Stinger. "I suppose you'll be telling us that that's the ship's cat! Well, let's just take a look."

The sack covering Sam was torn off and the boy and the dog were exposed. Then, with a deft flick of the wrist, Stinger pulled the sacking off Lucy and Hermione, and they too were revealed, crouched on the floor.

"Ah ha!" crowed Bert. "So, what have we here? Are these stowaways, my good Captain, or was you just lying to us all along?"

"Just leave them alone," said the Captain. "You've got what you came for. Now leave us alone."

Bert shook his head.

"Oh, no," he said. "I think that we might go away with rather more than we'd expected. What do you think?"

He turned to Stinger, who was a mean-looking man with a narrow face and lips that curled downwards in a constant snarl.

"We could do with a couple of extra hands in the galley," he said, pointing to Lucy and Hermione. "And as for that young man, he'd do fine for climbing up to the topsail. Boys like that can get places we can't get. They loves high rigging!"

"Good idea," said Bert. "Now let's just tie up the good Captain here. We don't want him getting any funny ideas about chasing us, does we?"

The children were powerless to help and Captain Foster, who did not want to do anything which could endanger the children, had no choice but to allow himself to be securely tied to his chair in the wheelhouse. Then, with a shout to the other pirates, Bert and Stinger led the children off to the side of the ship and tossed them, as if they were sacks of popcorn, on to the deck of the waiting pirate vessel.

The children huddled together miserably on the deck while the pirates busied themselves with getting their ship under sail. Then, when they were on their way, and pulling away from the sad sight of the drifting popcorn ship, the children were led by Stinger to Bert's cabin. Bert, it appeared, was the chief of the pirates, and he had the best cabin on board.

"Right," said Bert, in a businesslike voice, pointing to Lucy. "You two girls are to report to the galley. You tell Mrs Bert

that you're her assistants. It's your new
job. Now, let me see, what about pay?
You always gets told your pay when you
gets a new job. So, what are you land-
lubbers worth, eh? Ten hours work a day,
at . . . oooh, nothing an hour, makes . . ."

"Nothing, boss," said Stinger, laughing.

"Well done, Stinger," said Bert. "You was always very good at arithmetic. Pity you're so stupid at everything else."

Stinger laughed. "You're the one with the brains, Bert," he said cheerfully. "I always knew that."

"Thank you, Stinger," said Bert. "That's how I got where I am today. Brains. There's no substitute for brains, I say."

He turned to Sam, whose knees were knocking with fear, although he hoped it didn't show.

"Now you, young man. What's we got for you? Got a head for heights, have you? I hope so, because if you hasn't, then I'm afraid you're going to fall in. And pirate ships never goes back. If a man falls in, then it's the sharks for him, I'm sorry to say. I've seen many a man eaten by sharks, hasn't I, Stinger?"

"Oh, yes," said Stinger, smiling at the thought. "Old shark likes nothing better than a boy for breakfast. Or lunch, come to that."

"So you hold on to those ropes as tight as you can," said Bert. "Because if you doesn't, then it'll be as our friend Mr Stinger here says. Sharks."

Their interview with Bert at an end, the children were led off to their new jobs.

In the galley, Lucy and Hermione met Mrs Bert, who was a large lady in a striped apron. She had false teeth, which she kept in a glass beside the pots, and whenever she wanted to taste anything, she would have to put her teeth in first. She was not unkind to the girls, and told them that if they worked hard she would give them a piece of cake at the end of the day.

Sam was taken by one of the pirates to the mast and told to climb up and tighten some of the ropes. It was hard work, and the pirate in charge kept shouting at him when he made a mistake, but what was worst of all was the way the ship rocked backwards and forwards. When he was out on one of the cross-spars that held the sail, he could find himself dipping down towards the water at an alarming rate, only to be tipped heavenwards again before he knew where he was.

At the end of the day, Mrs Bert gave the children their meal at a table in the galley. They were almost too tired to eat, and Lucy and Hermione were longing for the hammocks which they had been given in a little cabin off the galley. Sam had not even been given a hammock; he had been told to sleep under a table in the galley, and a blanket had been placed there for him.

"Do you think we'll be rescued?" asked Hermione. "I can't bear the thought of being here for the rest of my life."

"I don't know," said Lucy. "I'm worried about Captain Foster. Will anybody find him in time, or will Biscuit know how to save him again? What if Biscuit can't get into the wheelhouse – what then?"

Hermione could not answer these questions, and nor could Sam. He had fallen asleep in his chair, and it was left to the two girls to lift him up gently and put him down on his blanket on the floor.

~ 6 ~
Stowaway

The children were all woken up at six o'clock the next morning and set to work. Lucy and Hermione were ordered to sweep out the galley and polish all the pots and pans. Sam was set to scrubbing the deck, a

71

back-breaking job that seemed to go on forever.

The pirates were delighted to have somebody to do this work for them, as they all seemed to be rather lazy. Bert sat in his cabin all day giving orders, Stinger walked around checking up that everybody was carrying out these orders, and the other four pirates, who were called Bill, Ed, Charlie and Tommy, liked nothing more than to lounge about on deck, whittling pieces of wood and spitting over the side of the railings.

They were a dreadful lot, thought Sam. Charlie had scars all over his face and arms – each of them from a different fight,

he explained — and Tommy had a mouth-
ful of blackened teeth and spiky stubble on
his chin. This made him look as if he had
swallowed a cactus, which wouldn't have
surprised Sam, as the pirate was always
eating whatever he could lay his hands
on — sugar cane, liquorice ropes and large
pieces of fudge specially made for him by
Mrs Bert. Bill and Ed did not look as bad
as the other two, but they both had six or
seven large gold rings in each ear, and this
made them rattle when they walked.

Sam was allowed to take a break from
his deck-scrubbing every now and then,
especially when Stinger was down below
and could not shout at him to work

harder. It was while he was having one of these rests, leaning against a large coil of rope, that he heard the sound that made his heart leap. It was not exactly a bark, but it sounded rather like one.

Sam turned round sharply. The sound seemed to be coming from the middle of the coil of rope and when he stood up and looked into it, his heart gave another leap. It was Biscuit! Sam put a finger to his lips and told Biscuit to keep quiet. The little dog seemed to understand, as he stopped his whining and lay down quietly where he was.

"Stay there!" Sam whispered to him. "Don't make a sound."

Sam looked around him. Stinger was nowhere to be seen and the other pirates seemed quite uninterested in what Sam was doing. Charlie was sharpening a knife, whistling cheerfully as he did so, and Tommy was sitting contentedly at the prow, eating a large piece of cake.

Sam made his way back along the deck and peered in through the galley door.

It was dark inside, and it took his eyes a few minutes to get accustomed to the darkness, but when they did he saw Lucy and Hermione sitting at a table, each polishing a pan.

"Psst!" said Sam. "Lucy! Psst!"

Lucy turned round and saw her brother at the door.

"It's all right," she whispered. "Mrs Bert's not here. You can come in."

Sam ran into the galley and told the two girls what he had seen.

"But how did he get there?" asked Hermione. "Did one of the pirates bring him?"

"No," said Lucy. "They just ignored him. I think that he must have jumped over on to their ship without their seeing him."

"Well, what are we going to do?" asked Sam. "If the pirates find him they might do something terrible. They might make him walk the plank or something like that."

"We'll smuggle him into our cabin," said Lucy. "They probably wouldn't find him there. Can you get him, Sam?"

Sam said he would try. He had an idea which he thought might work, and when he went back out on to the deck, the first thing he did was to walk over to one of the rails and look out to sea. After a while, he put his hand up to shade his eyes, as if he was trying to see something. Then, when he thought the time was right, he shouted out at the top of his lungs, "Ship ahoy! Coming our way fast!"

The pirates all sprang to their feet when they heard this and rushed over to where Sam was standing.

"Where?" shouted Tommy. "Where did you see this ship?"

"Over there," said Sam, pointing into the distance. "Over there! Look, I think that's its mast."

"Can't see a thing," snapped Charlie.

"The boy must have sharp eyesight," said Tommy. "Are you sure you saw a ship?"

"Yes," said Sam. "There it is! Can't you see it?"

"Go down and fetch Captain Bert," said Tommy. "Tell him there's a ship coming our way. We'll keep watch up here."

Sam slipped away from the pirates, who were all peering off into the distance with such interest that they would never

notice what he was doing. Returning to Biscuit's hiding place, he picked up the dog and ran back to the galley. Lucy and Hermione were still alone, and they took Biscuit from Sam and spirited him away to their cabin.

Sam now went down to Bert's cabin and knocked on the door. Bert's rough voice told him to enter, and when he went in, he found Bert and Stinger sitting round a table, drinking rum and playing cards.

"There's a ship coming our way," said Sam, saluting Bert as he spoke. "Mr Tommy said I was to warn you."

Bert and Stinger dropped their cards and pushed Sam out of the way as they rushed up to the deck. There, after a ten minute search of the sea with the telescope that Bert had stolen from Captain Foster, the pirate captain shook his head.

"You were right to raise the alarm," he said to Sam, patting him on the head. "Even if it's been a false one. You's got the making of a pirate, so you have. You work hard and one day you'll get a full-time job in the pirate trade, won't he, Stinger?"

Stinger tried to smile, but it came out all wrong. "Yes," he said. "As long as no sharks eat you before then, you'll probably grow up into a good pirate."

With these encouraging words, the two pirates returned to their game of cards, and life on the pirate ship went back to normal. The children, though, were all thinking of one thing. If Biscuit was on board, then Captain Foster would have had nobody to help him. And that meant that he could still be tied to his chair, with his boat drifting hopelessly at sea. They would have to do something soon, as there was not much time.

~ 7 ~
Lucy's Great Idea

The pirates were so pleased with all the hard work which the children had done that day that Bert agreed to let them stop early and have some time together on the deck before dinner. This was a mistake on Bert's part, because this was their chance to discuss what they could possibly do to get out of their terrible plight.

"We could try to take one of the rowing boats," said Sam. "We could lower it over the side and row away in the dead of night."

Lucy shook her head. "Not a good idea," she said. "We're too far from land by now and we wouldn't stand a chance of getting anywhere."

"We could put a bottle over the side with a message in it," ventured Hermione. "Somebody might pick it up and come to our rescue."

Again Lucy had to pour cold water on the idea. "It could be years before anybody found it," she said. "That would be far too late."

They were silent for a moment. Then Lucy smiled. "I'm beginning to get an idea," she said. "If you want to get the better of somebody, what do you do?"

She looked around for an answer, but nobody could think of anything to say.

"You think of their weak points," said Lucy. "And what are the weak points of these pirates?"

"They're greedy," said Sam. "Especially Tommy."

"Yes," said Lucy. "And did you see how those two with earrings ate – just like pigs? It's disgusting."

"And they're lazy too," said Hermione. "That's why they're pirates, rather than having an honest job."

"Precisely," said Lucy. "So we have a group of greedy, lazy pirates. At the moment, they're in control of the ship, but we want to take over. So what do we do?"

Again, neither of the others could think of an answer. So Lucy had to explain her idea to them. When she had done so, nobody spoke for a few moments. Then Hermione stood up and clapped her hands together.

"That is a brilliant idea," she exclaimed. "A wonderful, brilliant idea that is bound to work."

"Yes," said Sam, a little more hesitantly. "Very clever."

That evening, while the pirates were having their dinner, Lucy went up to their table and said that she had an announcement to make.

"Oh yes?" sneered Stinger. "What could you have to say that would possibly interest us?"

"Maybe they're going on strike," said Tommy. "Maybe they've had enough."

"Oh aye?" said Ed. "Well, if you don't like your job, you can always leave the ship. And we'll even provide a plank to help you on your way!"

The pirates all laughed at this joke, but Lucy did not mind.

"We wanted to do something for you," she said.

The pirates became silent.

"Do something for us?" said Bert. "Well, that's more like it, isn't it? What would this thing be?"

"We want to cook you some popcorn," said Lucy. "You see, this boat is full of popcorn, and we would like you to try just a little bit of it. We come from the Popcorn Islands, as you know, and nobody knows how to cook popcorn as well as a Popcorn Islander."

The pirates looked at one another. Greed: they could hardly resist the thought of a popcorn feast. And laziness: somebody else would be doing it for them.

"Well, I must say you children isn't too bad," said Bert. "Why don't you do that little thing for us. What do you say, men?"

The other pirates all nodded their agreement.

"Shall we do it for lunch tomorrow?" asked Lucy. "If you wouldn't mind giving us the morning off work, we'll get everything ready."

"Naturally," said Bert. "It's all in a good cause, of course. But you'll have to work twice as hard in the afternoon, mind you."

Lucy left them to the rest of their dinner and went back to the others.

"It's working," she said. "They fell for it. Now all we have to do is get everything ready tomorrow morning."

That night, as they lay in their hammocks – or on the galley floor, as the case may be – each of them thought of what was planned for the next day. It was a very daring plan, which might just work. Of course, if it didn't work . . . Well, that didn't bear thinking about.

The next morning Tommy accompanied the girls down into the hold of the pirate ship to get supplies of popcorn for the lunch.

"We'll need a whole sack," said Lucy, pointing to a particularly large sack of popcorn on top of all the others.

Tommy was a bit unsure, but his natural greed soon overcame his doubts.

"I suppose that's all right," he said, as he lifted the sack down on his broad shoulders and began to carry it to the galley. "I must say I can't wait to taste some of this stuff. I hope it's as good as you say it is, otherwise we shall all be very cross indeed and we may be tempted to throw you to the sharks."

Sam was waiting for them in the galley. They had it to themselves that morning, as Mrs Bert saw no reason to cook if there was going to be a popcorn feast for lunch. So the children did not even have to whisper as they made their preparations, and they were even able to bring Biscuit out of his hiding place to give him a chance to stretch his legs around the galley.

The first thing that they had to do was to move the cooking stove into the middle of the galley. This was not difficult, as the stove was on wheels, which could be locked into position once it was in the right place. Then, when the stove was ready, Sam and Lucy went off to the bathroom and carried back the large tin bath which the pirates used to wash in. This was given a good scrubbing and placed on top of the stove.

"Now all we have to do is to pour in the oil," said Lucy. "And then we can put the popcorn in."

The children went to the galley cupboard and took out several large bottles of cooking oil. These were poured into the tin bath, where they made a greasy, golden pool.

"Now," said Lucy. "Let's pour in the popcorn."

There's a very large amount of popcorn in a popcorn sack, and when they had finished, the tin bath was filled to the very brim with raw popcorn.

Lucy stood back and inspected their work. "I think we're ready," she said. "Let's put Biscuit back in the cabin and then we can sit down and wait until lunchtime."

There was only an hour or so to go before lunch, but it seemed to the children that the minutes were dragging by terribly slowly. Then, at last, the hands of the galley clock pointed to twelve o'clock and they knew that it was too late to back out.

~ 8 ~
A Lot of Popcorn

The pirates did not need to be reminded of the treat in store for them. At precisely twelve o'clock Tommy was at the galley door, where his eyes fell hungrily on the large tub of unpopped popcorn.

"Oh my goodness!" he cried, rubbing

his stomach in anticipation. "This looks very interesting!"

The others arrived shortly afterwards. Mrs Bert was the last to sit down, as she had some difficulty finding her teeth. But at last they were found in one of the frying pans and everybody was ready. They were all in a very good mood and were clearly looking forward to their unusual lunch.

"Makes a change from your potatoes, Mrs Bert," said Stinger.

Mrs Bert glared at him angrily. "Nothing wrong with my potatoes, is there, Bert?"

Bert smiled. "Nothing at all, my dear. But I must say that I does like a nice bit of popcorn now and then."

Lucy stepped forward and clapped her hands.

"Ladies and gentlemen," she began.

"Oh, that's a nice touch," said Bert. "They shows proper respect for their betters, these kids. I think it was a pretty good bit of work we did when we stealed . . . I mean, when we *invited* these kids on board."

Lucy waited until he had finished. Then she continued. "To thank you for all your kindness to us, we have prepared a traditional Popcorn Island feast for you. All I have to do is to light the stove and then, in a few minutes you will have all the delicious popcorn you could possibly eat!"

"Get on with it, then," said Bert impatiently. "We're all waiting."

Lucy stepped forward and lit the stove. Then the three children stood in the doorway and waited. The pirates all watched hungrily.

"I hope it doesn't take too long," said Tommy. "I didn't have a big breakfast this morning. I was saving myself for this."

"Excuse me," said Mrs Bert. "I saw you eating like a horse. You had four fried eggs and eight slices of toast. I saw you, Tommy. You can't fool me. Can you, Bert?"

"No," said Bert. "You can't fool Mrs Bert. I've tried for years, but it's never worked. You can't fool her."

While the pirates were arguing, the children were waiting for the first sounds of popping. Suddenly Sam nudged Lucy, and Lucy in turn nudged Hermione.

"It's started," Lucy whispered. "There it goes."

It is a special feature of popcorn from the Popcorn Islands that it explodes with a particularly loud pop. This started to happen all of a sudden, and the pirates let out whoops of delight. As some of the popped corn started to come to the surface, it was grabbed by eager hands and stuffed into eager mouths.

"Oh, this is wonderful!" mumbled Tommy, as he put handfuls of popcorn into his mouth.

This brought grunts of agreement from other popcorn-filled mouths. But now, as more popcorn exploded, something quite extraordinary happened. So much popcorn started to go off, popping and cracking like a hundred little fireworks, that it flowed over the edge of the tin tub. The pirates thought this was very exciting, and they got down on their hands and knees to scoop the popcorn off the floor. But they could not do it quickly enough. More popcorn went off, and still more after that. The galley was now beginning to fill up with popping popcorn, surrounding the pirates and completely hemming them in.

"Help!" shouted Mrs Bert suddenly. "Stop this popcorn! It's out of control!"

Nobody heeded her cries. The children certainly did not. They had now closed the galley door and were standing out on the deck, looking in through the window at the pirates. It was an unequal struggle they witnessed. No matter how hard the pirates tried to stand up and get out of the galley, they were forced back into their seats by exploding popcorn. It was like trying to swim in honey – quite impossible.

"It's worked!" shouted Hermione. "They're trapped!"

It was now a simple matter for Lucy to turn the key in the galley door and lock

the pirates in. They could do nothing to stop her, and they shouted and waved their fists angrily as they realised their plight.

"We'll get you!" shouted Stinger, from the middle of the great mound of popcorn which had surrounded him. "It'll be sharks for you!"

"Well it's popcorn for you!" shouted Sam in reply. "And it serves you right too!"

It was one thing to trap all the pirates, but quite another to take control of the ship. They would now have to try to turn it round and sail right back, hoping to reach the place where they had last seen Captain Foster. This would not be easy, as none of them knew a great deal about sailing, and the pirate ship was quite a large one.

"You go up and start pulling on those ropes," Lucy said to Sam. "Hermione and I will . . ."

She stopped. While everybody had been sitting down to their popcorn feast, the ship had continued on its way. This meant that the pirates must have left somebody in charge of the ship – somebody who was not in the galley!

Lucy quickly looked through the galley window. The room was now almost completely full of popcorn, and so it was difficult to tell exactly who was there. There was Bert – or a bit of him – and there were Stinger and Charlie, up to their necks in popcorn, and that arm over there, waving and pounding away to no effect, looked like a part of Bill. And of course Tommy could be made out in another pile of popcorn, or at least his stomach could. But there was no sign of Ed.

Lucy turned to Hermione and began to tell her what she had discovered.

"Ed must be at the ship's wheel," she said. "We should have thought –"

She was interrupted by an angry shout. There at the other end of the deck, shaking his fist in their direction, was Ed.

"What's going on?" he shouted. "Where's everybody? Why have you closed the galley door?"

The children stood stock still. Ed was now running towards them and nobody had any idea what to do. It would be impossible for them to resist him, as the pirates, even if lazy, were all remarkably strong. Ed would quickly overpower them and release the others, and then . . .

Biscuit leapt out and stood in front of Ed, growling and barking as fiercely as he could. Ed stopped where he was and looked down at the plucky little dog.

"Get out of my way, you stupid little animal," he snarled.

Biscuit did not take well to being talked to in this way, and he let out a low growl.

Ed now drew back a leg and aimed a hard kick in Biscuit's direction. With most dogs, that would have worked, but Biscuit, of course, moved sideways. Ed did not expect this, and suddenly found a determined little dog latched painfully on to his leg.

"Ow!" shouted Ed. "Get your dog off!"

Sam ran forward.

"Pull, Biscuit!" he shouted. "Pull as hard as you can."

Biscuit responded, and tugged ferociously on the pirate's leg. For a moment it looked as if he would just not have the strength to do it, but then, quite slowly,

Ed toppled over and landed with a crash on the deck. This gave Sam his chance. Seizing a coil of rope, he wrapped it round the dazed pirate and rolled him over and over, until he was completely tied up. Only then did Biscuit let go of Ed's leg.

Lucy and Hermione ran up to see that the hapless Ed was firmly secured. They were both experts in knots and they made quite sure that whatever Ed did, he would not be able to free himself.

Then they all looked at one another and smiled. The first stage of the plan had worked very well. They were very pleased with this, of course, but they all knew that a major test lay ahead.

~ 9 ~
Sailing
Homewards

Turning the ship round was not easy. With a sailing ship, you can't just turn the wheel and leave it at that – you have to allow the sails to fill with wind, and that is a fairly tricky piece of work. It is also quite dangerous. If you turn the wrong way, the ship can go right over on its side and capsize, and that's the end of the voyage.

Lucy took the wheel to begin with, while Hermione and Sam busied themselves with the sails. They had to prepare all the ropes and scurry up masts to make sure that the sails were all ready. Then, when Lucy gave the order, they had to pull hard on several ropes to bring the billowing sails under control.

When everything was ready, Lucy shouted out, "Ready about!" and everybody sprang into action. For a few moments the great ship seemed to lose speed as she turned into the wind, then, when the wind caught the sails again, everything began to tilt in an alarming way.

"Pull away!" Lucy shouted. "Haul in the sails!"

Sam and Hermione tugged and pulled for all their worth. At first it seemed as if they were getting nowhere, and the ship leaned further and further over. A few small waves came over the deck now, and lapped at their feet, but they did not let up. Slowly the sails came under control and the ship began to right itself.

"Well done!" shouted Lucy above the wind. "Now let's keep her like that."

They made good progress. There was a fresh wind behind them and the ship cut through the waves like a dolphin. Now that the sails were in the right position, Sam and Hermione had less to do, and they could sit on the deck, watching the blue ocean go by. Biscuit enjoyed the open air; he had been fed up with hiding in the cabin, and he was very happy to sit up on the prow, feeling the salt spray on his whiskers again.

Ed, of course, stayed exactly where he was, safely tied up on the deck, and in the galley the remaining pirates floundered hopelessly in their mounds of popcorn. Tommy had eaten quite a bit of it while he was trapped, and now had a well-deserved stomach ache. The others just passed their time in moaning and arguing about whose fault the whole thing was. Bert blamed Stinger, and Stinger blamed Bert, saying that he was not quite so clever as he had thought he was. Mrs Bert blamed both of them, and Bill thought it could all be put down to Mrs Bert's allowing the children to use the galley in the first place.

"And now we'll all be going to jail," moaned Bert. "That's a terrible end to a great career in piracy!"

"And I hear the food's not very good in jail," said Tommy. "Dry bread and things like that."

"Better than Mrs Bert's potatoes," said Bill. "I could never stand those potatoes, to tell the truth."

"You ate enough of them!" shouted Mrs Bert, pushing a heap of popcorn away from her face. "You never turned down second helpings."

And so it went on: moan, moan, bicker, bicker.

They sailed all afternoon and into the night. There was a bright moon out, and the children were perfectly able to see where they were going. Lucy handed over the helm to Hermione, and she in turn handed it over to Sam. So they all took turns in keeping the ship on course, all the way until morning.

By Lucy's calculations, they were now not too far away from the place where the pirates had first seized them. Sam was sent up to the crow's nest, the little basket up at the top of the highest mast, where he could sit and keep a lookout.

If he saw anything, he would shout out to the deck below and the ship could change course.

Sam's shout came about two hours after breakfast, which was some rather old ship's biscuit that they'd found in the hold. Lucy was at the helm and Hermione sitting on the deck below. They both

heard Sam's call, though, and looked up to see he was pointing.

"There she is!" shouted Sam. "I'm sure it's the popcorn ship."

Lucy swung the wheel round and Hermione and Sam adjusted the sails. There was a better wind in that direction, and the ship shot forward like a rocket. Soon they were close enough to confirm that it was indeed the popcorn ship, and a few minutes after that they lowered the sails and glided slowly up to the drifting ship. Biscuit, seeing his master's boat, was almost hysterical with excitement, and it was as much as the children could do to stop him from jumping overboard and swimming the last little distance. Then at last they were there, and they gently nudged up to the popcorn boat and tied their ship to its side.

Captain Foster was very tired, and very thirsty. "Quick," he said weakly, as they untied the rope around his chair. "Get me some lemonade from the cupboard."

He drank and drank, and then ate the ship's biscuit that they had saved for him.

"My goodness, I'm glad to see you," he said. "I had almost given up hope."

As the Captain recovered, they told him what had happened and revealed that the pirates were all safely tied or locked up on the ship next door.

"Well done," said Captain Foster. "Now all we have to do is to sail back to the island and tell them that all is well."

The last leg of the journey was not difficult. Hermione went on board the popcorn ship and Lucy and Sam stayed on the pirate ship. Biscuit, of course, stayed with his master, and kept a very close eye on him.

They sailed through the afternoon, and into the night. During the night, Lucy and Hermione flashed messages through the darkness to one another. This was very useful, as in this way Captain Foster was able to tell Lucy what to do.

"Captain Foster says you should pull your foresail in a bit," flashed Hermione.

"Aye, aye!" Lucy flashed back.

And then, when they were nearing the island harbour, and it was still dark, Hermione was able to flash the detailed instructions on how to make their way through the tricky channels that marked the harbour entrance.

Flash, *flash*, she signalled, which meant, "Go a little bit to starboard."

Or, *Double flash*, *flash*, *flash*, *half-flash*, which meant, "Captain Foster says you should look out for rocks on the port side."

Lucy made no mistakes, and when she finally brought the pirate ship safely into the harbour, Captain Foster and Hermione let out a great cheer from the popcorn ship. Then they tied up their boats, and stepped out on to dry land.

"We're home," said Lucy. "I can hardly believe it, but we've made it."

That morning, the news of what had happened spread round the island within minutes of sunrise. It also spread to the smaller islands, and soon people were flocking across by boat to see the captured pirate ship.

The children were terribly tired, but they were determined not to go to sleep just yet, and so they stayed down at the harbour to give their statements to the island policeman and to watch the pirates being arrested.

The pirates made a sorry spectacle. All of them, except for Ed, were covered in bits of popcorn and looked thoroughly miserable. The island policeman looked at them sternly, wrote their names in his notebook, and then put handcuffs on them to prevent them from running away.

"What will happen to them now?" Lucy asked Captain Foster.

"They'll go to jail," said the Captain. "And they'll stay there until Christmas. Then, if they promise to give up piracy and take an honest job somewhere, they may be allowed to go free."

*

And I'm happy to say, that is what they did. Every single one of them, including the dreadful Stinger, became very sorry for what they had done, and all of them got honest jobs and became decent citizens. Bert was given a job as captain of a pirate ship in a theme park (not a real pirate ship, of course), and Mrs Bert took a job making hot dogs for the visitors. Bill, Ed, Charlie and Tommy all got jobs in Hollywood as actors in pirate films, and indeed they became quite famous for this. But they never forgot their promise to be good, and in fact they gave quite a lot of money to build a home for old sailors.

And as for Stinger, well nobody thought he would ever succeed in keeping an honest job for long, but he did. He became a shark scarer at a famous beach. Whenever a shark was sighted getting too close to the swimmers, Stinger would go out in his little boat and then jump into the sea near the shark. At the sight of the dreadful Stinger, with his frightening face and his mean look, the shark would usually turn tail and flee. It was a job that suited Stinger perfectly, as he was always happy when snarling, and snarling at sharks is as snarly a job as anyone can imagine. Of course it was possible that one day he might meet a shark who wasn't frightened of him, but then that's another story, and no job can be perfect in all respects.

But what about the Popcorn Islands? Well, life there returned to normal, and Captain Foster continued to carry the popcorn off to market and the islanders continued to grow it. There was one change, though. At the trial of the pirates, which took place on a much bigger, more important island, the judge declared that under the law of piracy, a pirate ship belonged to the person who captured it!

"So," said the judge, "I now declare that the pirate ship currently lying in the harbour of the Popcorn Islands is the property for all time, and forever hereafter and theretofore, and all the rest, of those three brave children, namely, to wit, those herewith described."

Judges have a very grand way of speaking, and what he really meant to say was that the pirate ship now belonged to Lucy, Hermione and Sam.

They were delighted by this, and they spent a great deal of their spare time polishing the decks and making sure that everything was in good order. Then, when visitors arrived, which they did from time to time, they were given a marvellous tour of the islands by the three children on their pirate ship. And when he had his holidays, which he now always spent on the Popcorn Islands, Captain Foster would give sailing courses in the pirate ship for all the local children.

These were great fun. At the end of each day – after a busy sail in the great ship – the children would sit on the deck with Captain Foster, and Biscuit of course, and drink lemonade. Then popcorn would be served – crisp, delicious Popcorn Island popcorn – of which no one ever gets tired. And as the sun would sink over the horizon into the sea, Captain Foster and the children would often chat about their adventure with the popcorn pirates, and agree that it would make a wonderful story, if somebody ever cared to write it all down . . .

THE BUBBLEGUM TREE

~ 1 ~
In the Bubblegum Works

Have you ever visited a bubblegum factory? No? Neither had Billy, even though there was one right on the edge of his town. There it stood – the Better Bubblegum Works – with its tall chimney and its two very grand gates, both painted bubblegum pink.

This factory was run by a man called Mr Walter Alliwallah Pravindar Gopal, usually just called Mr Gopal, or even Walter. Mr Gopal was a well-known man in the town, and very popular with everybody. As he walked down the street, people would say, "Good morning, Mr Gopal. Fine day, isn't it?"

Mr Gopal would beam at them in a very friendly manner and say, "Excellent day! Oh, yes it is! Very fine indeed!" And as often as not, he would reach into his pocket and offer them a stick of Gopal's Best Pink Bubblegum, wonderfully fresh from the factory. People liked this.

Billy and his sister, Nicola, always greeted Mr Gopal very politely, and were usually rewarded with a stick or two of bubblegum. They thought Mr Gopal was quite the friendliest person they had ever met and were both very proud that he had chosen their town in which to build his famous factory.

Then, one day, Billy saw Mr Gopal walking down the street, shaking his head and looking rather sad.

"Good morning, Mr Gopal," said Billy. "It's a nice day, isn't it?"

Mr Gopal looked at Billy sadly. "I am sorry to say, Billy," he began, "that even if it's a nice day, I'm not enjoying it at all. Dear me!"

Billy was astonished. Nobody had ever known Mr Gopal to look sad. There must be something very seriously the matter.

"Is there something wrong at the factory?" he asked.

"Yes," said Mr Gopal, shaking his head again. "There is something very wrong at the factory, and if you come along with me I shall show you exactly what it is."

Billy was excited to be going into the bubblegum factory, even if Mr Gopal seemed in such a sad mood. As he accompanied Mr Gopal through the front door, he smelled the wonderful smell of bubblegum – a smell like no other smell. It was a pink sort of smell – a smell that seemed to get bigger as you smelled it and then burst, just like the popping of a bubble.

"This way," said Mr Gopal. "We shall go to my office."

Billy followed Mr Gopal past the great bubblegum-making machines, all humming and whirring away in a most energetic fashion. It was all very interesting to see, but Billy was worried and could not enjoy himself as much as he would have liked.

Mr Gopal showed Billy into his office and sat him down on a chair.

"Here," he said, taking a piece of bubblegum from a tray on his desk. "This is a piece of bubblegum, is it not?"

"Yes," said Billy, looking at the stick of Gopal's Best.

"I'd like you to unwrap it," said Mr Gopal, passing the stick to Billy.

"Then pop it in your mouth and chew hard."

Billy was rather puzzled, but did as he was told. He slipped the pink stick out of its silver paper and put it into his mouth. Then he began to chew. It tasted fine, and the smell – well, that was exactly the same as it always was.

"Now," said Mr Gopal. "I'd like you to blow a bubble. Just an ordinary bubble."

Billy moved the gum around his mouth, getting it to just the right place for blowing a bubble. Then he blew.

He blew hard. Then he blew again. A moment or two later a small bit of gum popped out of his mouth, and a tiny, almost invisible bubble appeared. Then it burst – with a little pop, like a frog's hiccup – and was gone.

Billy sucked the gum back in. "I'll try again," he said. "That wasn't very good."

"Oh dear," said Mr Gopal, wringing his hands. "It won't make any difference. You can try and try again, it'll be the same. You won't do any better than that."

Mr Gopal was right. Try as he might, Billy could not blow a proper bubble. There was something very badly wrong with the gum.

"It's hopeless," said Mr Gopal. "The gum just isn't the same as it used to be."

"But what's gone wrong?" asked Billy, dropping the useless bubblegum into the bin. "Why won't it work?"

"It's a very strange story," said Mr Gopal. "Would you like me to tell you all about it?"

"Yes," said Billy, feeling very sorry for the dejected bubblegum manufacturer. "Maybe I can help."

So Mr Gopal told Billy about what had happened. And it was indeed a very strange tale -- stranger than anything Billy had heard before.

~ 2 ~
A Very Strange Story

"I got the recipe for my bubblegum from my father," began Mr Gopal. "He was a very famous bubblegum manufacturer in his time – even more famous than I am. He lived in India, in a town called Bombay, which is a marvellous, exciting place, I can tell you.

"He had a big bubblegum factory where he used to make a bubblegum called Bombay Best Bubbly. His business was a great success, but I'm sorry to say that one day a terrible fire burned the whole factory down – right to the ground. Nobody knew how it started, but it destroyed all my father's property and he lost just about everything he had in this life. It even burned my father's moustache off. It had been a wonderful moustache; now it was just a tiny, scorched line.

"So from being a rich man, my father became a poor man. Fortunately, there were one or two possessions which he kept away from the factory, at home. These included an old black money box with two thousand rupees in it, and a small black book which he always hid under his pillow. That was about all.

"I remember the day after the fire, when my father came back to the house and called me into the front room. He stood there, with his sad moustache, and his eyes all watering from the smoke.

" 'I am an old man,' he said. 'And I want to say something very important to you. You are my only child, Walter Alliwallah Pravindar Gopal, and you are all I am going to leave behind in the world. So I just want to say this to you.

Remember that a Gopal is always a brave man — always — and there is nothing he is scared to do. Your grandfather, Sikrit Pal Praviwallah Gopal, was not even frightened of tigers and fought one with his bare hands when it attacked him. He bit its tail so hard that the tiger jumped off his back and retreated into the jungle. That isn't at all unusual for a Gopal. That is how a Gopal behaves.

" 'The second thing I want to say to you is this. Now that I am a poor man, I cannot leave you great riches on this earth. All I have is this box of a few rupees and this book. Use the rupees to go off and make your fortune, and use what is in the book to start a great bubblegum factory again. Remember that the Gopals have always been bubblegum people.'

"And with that my father gave me the box and the book. Then he reached out and touched me lightly on the head, went into his room, and put on a simple white robe. After that, he said goodbye to me, shook my hand, and walked out of the house.

"I watched him walk down the path from the house and then off on to the dusty road. People do that in India. When they reach a certain time of life, they sometimes just walk off and become holy men and never come back. That is what my father did.

"My eyes were filled with tears as I watched him go. I knew, though, that this was what he wanted to do – his heart, you see, was broken when his factory burned down. Then, a short while later I set off on my own travels. These eventually brought me here – to this town – where I worked hard, day and night, until I had saved enough money to build the bubblegum factory in which you are sitting right at this very moment."

Mr Gopal was silent for a moment, and Billy wondered whether he had come to the end of his story. But he had not.

"You will be asking yourself, Billy, *What was in that book?* Well, I shall tell you.

"When I opened the book, I had a great surprise. I don't know quite what I had expected to find inside, but all that I saw was line after line of writing that made no sense at all. My father, you must realise, had written the whole thing in code, and he had forgotten to give me the key!

"So I sat and looked at the meaningless jumble of letters and tried to make some sense of it. What on earth could *momixaying bomowl* mean? And why did the word *gomum* keep appearing? I was quite at a loss as to what to do, and so I just carried the little book around with me, tucked away in my inside pocket.

"Then a short while later, on a long train journey from Bombay, I found myself sitting opposite a man who was busy doing a crossword puzzle. It was a hot afternoon, and I was half asleep as the train chugged along on its journey. But then, as my eyes rested on my fellow passenger, I was brought back to wakefulness by the sheer speed with which he was solving the clues. His pencil seemed to dart across the paper like a bird, filling in the letters, and in no time at all he had finished the puzzle.

"I sat bolt upright.

" 'Excuse me, sir,' I said. 'I noticed that you were very quick in solving that puzzle. I wonder if you could help me.'

"The other man looked at me over the glasses that were perched on the tip of his nose.

" 'You are addressing Mr P.J. Lal,' he said, 'the crossword puzzle champion of all India. If it is a crossword clue that is worrying you, then you are undoubtedly speaking to the right man.'

"I was encouraged by his helpfulness, and I immediately took out my little book and opened it before him.

" 'This was given to me by my father,' I said. 'And he did not give me the key to his code. It contains something I am very keen to read.'

"Mr P.J. Lal took the book from me and examined the writing. 'May I ask you what your father's name was?' he said.

"I told him, and he wrote the letters of his name out on a strip of paper. Then the stub of pencil darted about, scribbling other letters underneath and moving them about. I watched in fascination and was very disappointed when, after several minutes, Mr P.J. Lal shook his head.

"'And what was the name of your grandfather?' he asked.

"I told him, and on another strip of paper he wrote out, in large letters: SIKRIT PAL PRAVIWALLAH GOPAL. Again there was much scribbling as he juggled with letters. Then he shook his head once more.

"'May I ask where your father was born?' he said.

" 'Bombay, of course,' I replied.

"Mr P.J. Lal looked thoughtful for a few moments, but then he burst out laughing.

" 'Very simple,' he said. 'Take the Bs out of Bombay and you get OM and AY, do you not?'

"He did not wait for me to answer.

" 'Put an OM before each vowel – that is before any A, E, I, O or U. Then put an AY before the next vowel, and there you are.'

"I was not sure what he meant, and so he leaned forward and showed me.

" '*Bubblegum* becomes BOMUBB-LAYEGOMUM,' he explained. 'And these words, MOMIXAYINGBOMOWL, are simply mixing bowl. Do you see what I mean?'

"I had to agree. It was quite simple, and now, with a little effort, I could read what my father had written.

"I looked up to thank Mr P.J. Lal, but he was already on his feet, reaching for his suitcase, as we were arriving at a station. He smiled at me, put his hat on his head, and disappeared, and I am always sorry that I could not have rewarded him in some way for what he did. But I had the key to the code now, and for the rest of the journey I sat and read the very strange story which my father had written down."

~ 3 ~
The Story of the Bubblegummies

"Was it a recipe?" asked Billy.

"Yes," said Mr Gopal. "There was a recipe. But there was much more besides. My father, you see, not only told me what to put in the bubblegum, but where to get the ingredients."

Billy was puzzled. "Can't you just buy them from a supermarket – like anything else?"

"Oh, you can do that if you want to make just any old bubblegum," said Mr Gopal. "But if you want to make real bubblegum, bubblegum that remains wonderfully chewy for days and days, you have to put something very special in it." Mr Gopal paused. "Can you keep a secret, Billy?"

Billy nodded. He had always been good at keeping secrets, even those that were really very difficult to keep.

"In that case," said Mr Gopal, "I shall tell you what was in that book.

"My father told me that right back in the days when he started his factory, one of the men who worked there came to his office. This man, who came from a remote part of India – a place where there are still great jungles and empty hills – told my father that he had something which would make his bubblegum even better. So my father asked him to show it to him.

"The man took a square of a rubbery pink substance out of his pocket. He handed it to my father and said, 'This is from the bubblegum tree which grows in our jungle at home. If you add it to your bubblegum, it will make it the finest in the world.'

"Of course, my father did not believe him at first, but when he examined the curious, rubbery square, it smelled so good that he decided to try it. And it worked, just as the man said it would. It made the bubblegum wonderfully soft and chewy. So there must be a bubblegum tree after all!

"Well, my father was thrilled. And he was even more thrilled when the man told him that the people he knew up in the jungle would send a regular supply of this new raw gum, which they did. And in return, every month, my father sent money to repay them for their trouble. These people, he said, were called the

Bubblegummies, and they seemed very friendly and gentle people indeed.

"My father wrote in his book exactly how to get in touch with the Bubblegummies – he even drew a map – and he also explained just how much gum should go into the mixture. And so, when I opened my own bubblegum factory, I wrote to these people, and received a very friendly letter back from them.

"They said that they were very sorry to hear about my father's fire, and that they would be quite happy to send me squares of raw gum whenever I needed them.

"And that's why my bubblegum has always been so chewy – and tasted so

good as well. Every month without fail,
a parcel has arrived from India with
supplies of the gum. Then, two months
ago, the parcel failed to turn up, and since
then I have heard nothing from the
Bubblegummies – nothing at all. I wrote
to them, of course, but the post office

from which they used to collect their mail sent my letter back to me. Nobody had collected it, they said.

"And that, Billy, is why you see me looking so sad. I am very worried that something has happened to the Bubblegummies."

After Mr Gopal had told this story, they both sat silently for a little while. Then at last Billy spoke.

"Why don't you go and find out what's happened?" he asked. "Maybe there's a very simple explanation."

Mr Gopal looked at him in astonishment. "Do you mean – go to the jungle?"

Billy nodded. "Yes," he said. "Surely somebody would be able to take you there."

Mr Gopal stared at Billy. "But I couldn't possibly do that," he protested. "Oh no. I couldn't possibly go off to the jungle all by myself. There are . . . well, there are tigers and things like that out there." As he spoke, he gave a slight shudder.

Billy thought for a moment. "You could go with somebody," he said. "You needn't go alone."

"But I don't know anybody who would want to go to the jungle," wailed Mr Gopal. Then he paused, looking hard at Billy. "You wouldn't help me, would you, Billy? You wouldn't come to the jungle with me?"

Billy gave his answer immediately. "Of course I'd come. And my sister Nicola would come too. We'd both come with you."

Mr Gopal heaved a sigh of relief. "Well, in that case, I shall be happy to go. We should make plans immediately."

"There's one problem," said Billy. "India's a very long way away. How shall we get there?"

Mr Gopal only had to think for a moment. "That will be quite simple," he said. "I have an aunt who has a flying boat."

"A flying boat?" asked Billy.

"Yes," said Mr Gopal. "It's a very old aeroplane that used to fly all the way out to India, landing on lakes and the sea on the way. It's a funny old plane, but I'm sure that Aunty would be quite delighted to have an excuse to get it going again."

Then Mr Gopal stopped, as if he had suddenly found a flaw in their plan.

"Will your parents let you go?" he asked doubtfully. "Some parents would get very worried about their children going off to India in flying boats. You know how parents are. Do you think yours are like that?"

"Not at all," said Billy. "I'm sure that they'll say yes – if you agree to bring us back safely."

Mr Gopal nodded. "It will be a great adventure," he said. "But I'm sure that it's the sort of adventure that one comes back from safe and sound. So why not go and ask them right now? Then we can get everything ready."

Billy was right about his parents.

"Off to India?" said his father, when he told him of Mr Gopal's invitation. "In a flying boat? Sounds like a splendid idea to me! I wish I could come too, but I'm just too busy at the moment."

And the children's mother said much the same thing.

"The jungle!" she exclaimed. "What a wonderful adventure! Of course you can go. But promise me you'll be extremely careful of snakes and tigers and things like that."

~ 4 ~
Off to India!

It was a wonderful trip. With Mr Gopal reading the maps, and his aunt at the controls, the faithful old plane droned its way across mountains, plains, and long stretches of sea. Nicola and Billy passed sandwiches around and poured tea for everybody from large flasks which they had brought with them. And from time to time they slept, although it was generally far too exciting to do much of that.

They had to stop every now and then, to fill the tanks of the plane and to allow Mr Gopal's aunt to have a rest. They landed in Egypt, on the river Nile, and watched the white-sailed boats drift by. Then they landed on the sea beside a desert, and watched the camels plod their way over the sand dunes at the water's edge. And finally, after several days of travel, Mr Gopal looked up from his map and announced that unless he was mistaken – which of course he wasn't – the smudge of land down below them was the coast of India.

They still had some way to go, as the jungle they were looking for was quite a distance from the coast. But Mr Gopal's map was very accurate, and he guided his aunt right to the very river where they could land the flying boat. She landed the plane perfectly, hardly making a ripple on the water, and there they were, on the river at the edge of the jungle.

The engines of the plane stopped and the propellers came to a halt. It was terribly quiet now, after the roar of the engines had died away, and the jungle seemed very thick.

"Are you sure we're in the right place?" asked Billy. "It all seems very deserted to me."

"One hundred per cent sure," said Mr Gopal. "Or almost . . ."

They stared out of the window of the plane. The edge of the river was lined with great trees, which seemed to get even taller further away. It looked as if it would be very difficult to go anywhere in jungle as thick as that. But then Mr Gopal gave a cry.

"There it is!" he said. "Over there. A clearing – in just the place the map said it would be!"

They tied the plane to a tree at the water's edge. Then carefully looking

where they were putting their feet, they stepped out of the plane and into the grassy clearing.

"I think we should sit down and have a cup of tea," said Mr Gopal's aunt, producing a flask. "It's been a very long flight."

The children were keen to start exploring, but they knew that there would be plenty of time for that. So they all sat down and sipped at their tea while they looked at the jungle around them. From close up, it seemed even thicker than it had looked from the window of the plane, and they wondered how they could possibly find anybody in all that greenery.

Suddenly Billy reached out and tapped Nicola on the arm. "Don't stare too hard," he whispered, "but I'm quite sure that that bush over there moved!"

Nicola followed his gaze to a large bush at the edge of the clearing. "You must be imagining things," she whispered back. "It's just a bush."

And at that moment, the bush moved again. It did not move far, but it moved, and both children gave a start.

"Mr Gopal," whispered Billy. "There's a moving bush —"

He did not have time to finish. The bush now dashed across the clearing, making for the far side.

"Mr Gopal!" shouted Billy. "Look at that bush!"

As he called out, Billy leapt up and stuck out his leg, right in the way of the moving bush. There was a grunt, followed by a muffled cry, and over went the bush in a shower of leaves. Then, from the middle of the fallen bush, there emerged a rather tall man.

He looked at Billy. "You really should be more careful," he said. "I could have taken a painful fall."

"I'm sorry," said Billy. "I thought you were just a bush. I didn't know . . ."

The man turned away, looking rather annoyed, and spoke to Mr Gopal.

"And who may you be?" he asked directly.

"I am Walter Alliwallah Pravindar Gopal," said Mr Gopal.

The man seemed very surprised. "Oh!" he exclaimed. "Do you mean you are *the* Walter Alliwallah Pravindar Gopal?"

"I believe so," said Mr Gopal.

The man broke into a smile. "In that case, I needn't even have bothered to spy on you at all! So you are Walter Alliwallah Pravindar Gopal! Well, well, well!"

"Are you one of the Bubblegummies?" asked Mr Gopal.

The man nodded enthusiastically and began to shake hands with everybody.

"I am Mr Bhalla," he said. "And you are all very welcome. I'm sorry that I seemed so suspicious to begin with. Please, come with me. I can't say we were expecting you, but everybody will be very pleased that you have arrived."

They followed the man along a path through the jungle. Billy had never been in a jungle before, and found it very strange and delicious to be walking through the green light that filtered down from above. He noticed the trailing vines, and the orchids, and the broad-

leaved ferns. He noticed the butterflies —
bigger than any he had ever seen before —
and the twisted roots of the great
trees. It was an intriguing, wonderful
place.

"Almost there," called out Mr Bhalla
after a while. "Just a little way to go."

The jungle had now thinned out, and
they seemed to be reaching the edge of a
plain, with dotted trees, and mountains
in the distance.

"We don't actually live in the
jungle itself," said Mr Bhalla. "We prefer
to be just on the edge. And now, if you
look closely, you'll see our place up
ahead."

They all looked ahead. There was a lot of grass, and a large cluster of tall trees, but nothing else.

"I can't see any houses," said Mr Gopal's aunt. "Are you sure we've come the right way?"

"Ah," said Mr Bhalla, smiling broadly. "Perhaps you should look up a bit rather than down."

They looked up, and it was Nicola who saw it first. "Look," she cried, pointing at the trees. "There's a house!"

"That's right," said Mr Bhalla. "That's my brother's house, actually. Mine is a bit further on, in that large tree with the bushy top. And over there, at the far end, is the school. And the hospital is over there. It has two trees all to itself."

Billy was astonished, and as they drew closer to the trees, his astonishment grew. The Bubblegummies had made an entire village in the trees! Craning his neck,

Billy could see just how skilfully they had made it. Each house, which was beautifully fashioned out of wood, was connected to the tree next to it by a wooden walkway, and that tree would be connected to the tree beyond, and so on. There were ladders, too, which led from level to level, and swinging bridges, knotted with vines, crossing the wider spaces. You could live entirely in the trees, it seemed.

Mr Bhalla led them to the bottom of a large tree, looked up into the branches, and whistled. For a moment nothing happened, and he whistled again. Then, out of the thick leaves above, there appeared a long ladder, being lowered slowly down to them.

"Please," he said, gesturing politely. "Please climb up here."

~ 5 ~
Bungee Jumping

"This is my house," said Mr Bhalla, when they reached the top of the ladder. "Please come in."

They followed him into the tree house, and found themselves in a large room filled with colourful furniture. Mr Bhalla asked them to sit down, and then went off to fetch refreshments.

"Now, what is the trouble?" asked Mr Gopal, as they sipped at long glasses of a delicious pink sherbet drink which Mr Bhalla had given them.

Mr Bhalla put down his glass. "If you come to this window, you'll see," he said.

They crossed the room, which was swaying gently as the tree moved with the breeze. Mr Bhalla opened a window and pointed to the edge of the jungle.

"Our bubblegum trees grow on the edge of the jungle," he said. "They're very old trees. Each tree has to grow for at least a hundred years before it gives any gum.

Fortunately, nobody ever thought of cutting them down before, and so we've had a good number of trees. But now . . ."

Billy looked out of the window towards the jungle. Was that a plume of smoke in the distance? Or was it a cloud?

"Do you mean somebody is cutting them down?" asked Mr Gopal, sounding shocked.

"Yes," said Mr Bhalla. "They are. It started a few months ago. Some men came and set up camp further up the river. Then they started to cut down our trees. They have wonderful wood, you see – there's nothing else quite like it. The men cut down our trees and float them down the river to a sawmill."

Billy was outraged. "But they're your trees!" he exclaimed. "You've always looked after them!"

Mr Bhalla sighed. "We think they're our trees, but these men say otherwise. We've tried to stop them, but they've just run after us with their axes and chased us away. There's nothing we can do. Maybe it would be different if we were different people, but Bubblegummies don't like fighting – we never have."

Mr Bhalla returned to his chair and sank his head in his hands. "So that's why you haven't been getting your gum," he said. "And if things go on as they are, in a few months the men will have cut all the trees down and that will be the end of the bubblegum tree – forever."

Nobody said anything. Billy thought that he had never heard such a sad story before. Surely somebody could think of something? Surely somebody could do something to save the bubblegum trees before it was too late.

Mr Bhalla invited them all to stay, and showed them to their rooms in his tree house. Then, since they had a few hours before dinner, Billy and Nicola set off to explore the Bubblegummie village.

It was a marvellous, exciting place.

Everybody was very friendly, and when they met some children coming out of the school, their new friends quickly agreed to show them round. They took them along all the walkways and swinging bridges, and even showed them up the lookout ladders that led to the very tops of the trees.

"Why do you live in tree houses?" asked Billy.

"Why not?" said one of the Bubble-gummie boys. "Wouldn't you prefer to live in a tree house?"

"I suppose I would," said Billy. "You get a much better view. And it's cooler. And your house would never get flooded in the rain."

"That's it," said the boy. "That's why we live up here."

Most exciting of all, though, was the emergency exit. This was right in the middle of the village, at the top of one of the tallest trees, and it was shown to Billy and Nicola by the Bubblegummie boy.

"We have to have a way of getting down to the ground in a hurry," he said. "Like if somebody fell, or if there were a fire. This is what we do."

He showed them to a platform to which a thick pink rope was tied. "You hold the end of this rope," he said, "and then you jump."

Billy inspected the rope. It had a very strange feel to it.

"This feels like bubblegum," he said.

"And that's just what it is," said the boy. "We use bubblegum for all sorts of things."

He took the end of the rope from Billy's hand. "Let me show you," he said. "Please stand back."

Billy and Nicola watched as the boy tucked the end of the rope into his belt. Then, without any further warning, he leapt over the edge of the platform.

The two children gave a gasp as they saw the boy plummet down.

"He's going to hit the ground!" screamed Nicola. "Oh, look out!"

But Nicola was wrong. The long bubblegum rope unravelled swiftly, but then stopped, and began to stretch. It was just like a great piece of elastic, and it brought the boy to a stop just before he hit the ground. Then, with a loud twanging noise, the rope jerked him back up, shooting through the air, to land on his feet on the platform.

"There you are," said the boy. "It's quite simple. If I had wanted to get off at the bottom, I would just have slipped the rope out of my belt. But it's just as easy to come back up again."

Billy laughed. "It's just like bungee jumping!" he exclaimed.

"Of course it is," said the boy. "We invented bungee jumping, you see. The Bubblegummies were the first to do it — not that anybody knows about that!"

He passed the end of the rope to Billy. "Would you like to try?" he asked. "It's very simple."

Billy's heart gave a leap. The ground was a very long way away. What if the bubblegum rope broke?

"I'm not sure," he stammered. "Maybe tomorrow . . ."

"I'll go," said Nicola, reaching for the rope. "It looks like great fun."

Billy held his breath as Nicola launched herself into space. He would get into terrible trouble, he thought, if the rope broke, and he had to take Nicola home all covered in plaster. But it did not, and within seconds his sister was back up on the platform, beaming with pleasure. After that, Billy had to do it himself, and he found it just as easy as the boy had said. So they each had one more jump, and then it was time to get back to Mr Bhalla's for dinner. The sun was going down now, and night was falling on the jungle.

Mr Bhalla had prepared a magnificent meal of coconut rice, and there was more of the pink sherbet drink which they had all enjoyed so much earlier on. Then, because they were all tired from the journey, they decided it was time to go to bed.

As he prepared to go off to his room, Billy took Mr Bhalla aside. "Are there many wild animals here?" he asked.

Mr Bhalla smiled. "You don't have to be worried, Billy," he said reassuringly. "You're perfectly safe up in the trees. The most we get up here is the odd monkey now and then."

"But what about in the jungle?" Billy pressed. "Are there any . . . any tigers?"

Mr Bhalla shook his head. "No tigers, I'm afraid. There used to be, many years ago, but they moved on. So don't worry about that."

Billy thought for a moment.

"If there were tigers a long time ago," he said quietly, "does anybody in the village have a tiger skin?"

Mr Bhalla looked at Billy in surprise. "What a strange question! But as a matter of fact, they do. We have three or four altogether. I have a very old one which my grandfather gave to me before he died. And there are a few others. But why do you ask?"

"I've had an idea," said Billy. "I've had

an idea about how to help you. I'm not sure whether it will work, but there's no harm in trying."

Mr Bhalla looked at Billy, and for a moment it seemed as if his eyes would fill with tears.

"If it might save our trees," he said, "then anything – *anything* – is worth trying."

~ 6 ~
Billy's Plan:
Part One

The next day, over a tasty breakfast of poppadoms and marmalade, Billy told everybody about his plan.

"Our only hope," he said, "is to scare those men away. If they become too frightened to work in the jungle, then they'll leave."

"And the trees will be saved," interrupted Nicola.

"Exactly," said Billy.

There was a silence while everybody thought about this. There was no doubt it was true; but there was something which still needed to be explained.

It was Mr Gopal who asked the question which everybody was pondering.

"But how do we frighten them away?" he asked. "It's easy to say that you will frighten somebody, but how do you do it? Those men sound pretty fierce from what Mr Bhalla has told us."

Billy smiled. "They may be fierce, but there's something much fiercer than they are."

"I don't understand," said Mr Gopal, shaking his head.

"Nor do I," said his aunt. "I don't see how we could frighten people like that."

"We might not be able to frighten them," said Billy. "But what about tigers? Wouldn't they frighten them away?"

Mr Gopal snorted. "Of course they would," he said. "But where are the tigers going to come from?"

Billy smiled. This was the funny part of the plan.

"You'll see," he said. "But first, we have to go off and have a word with these men. Just you and I will go, Mr Gopal. The others must stay behind and get ready for tonight."

Once Billy had explained the rest of the plan, Mr Gopal was full of enthusiasm.

"What a brilliant idea!" he cried. "Oh, Billy, well done! I certainly wouldn't like to be in those men's shoes this evening!"

Together they climbed down the ladder from Mr Bhalla's house, while the others waved farewell from above. Then, following the well-worn path that led to the bubblegum trees, they set off purposefully on their errand.

As they got closer to the trees, they heard a sound which made their blood run cold. It was the sound of an axe chopping away at wood.

"Listen to that," said Billy angrily. "That's a tree being cut down."

"I know," said Mr Gopal. "What a terrible waste of a bubblegum tree. A hundred years being thrown away – just like that."

They followed the sound and in a few minutes, as they rounded a bend in the path, they heard a voice shout out ahead of them.

"Timber!" it yelled. "Down it comes!"

Billy and Mr Gopal stopped short. A giant tree was coming down – but where would it land? Suddenly, there was a great crashing sound, and the sky above them seemed for a moment to be blotted out by a canopy of leaves and branches.

"Mr Gopal!" shouted Billy. "Run!"

Mr Gopal was confused, but Billy grabbed him by the shirtsleeve and tugged him off the path. He was just in time, for had he not done so, Mr Gopal would have been crushed by the great tree as it fell.

"Thank you," said Mr Gopal, wiping his brow. "That was a very close shave. If you hadn't pulled me away like that . . ."

He did not finish the sentence. Angry voices could now be heard, and within a few moments the two of them found themselves surrounded by men with axes in their hands and red handkerchiefs tied round their foreheads.

"What are you doing here?" snapped the tallest of the men. "You could have got yourself killed then! You should keep away from logging, you know!"

"I'm very sorry," said Mr Gopal. "But my young friend here and I are on a very important mission. We certainly didn't want to disturb you."

The polite tone of Mr Gopal's words seemed to make the man a bit calmer, and when he next spoke he sounded less angry.

"Well, just watch out in future," he said. "What do you want, anyway?"

Mr Gopal glanced at Billy, who now
stepped forward to speak.

"Mr Gopal here is a famous photo-
grapher," he said. "And we have come
from a very long way away to photograph
some animals which we have been told
are to be found in this part of the jungle.

206

That is why we are here."

The man looked at Billy and sneered. "Well, you're wasting your time," he said. "There's nothing of any interest in this jungle."

"Except for tigers," said Billy quickly.

"What did you say?" said the man sharply.

"Tigers," said Billy. "Big tigers. They're very fierce, these ones, we believe – and very rare."

This was the signal for all the men to burst out laughing.

"What nonsense," said one of them. "There are no tigers here! There aren't any tigers for miles. We should know."

"But you must be wrong," said Billy. "We've been told that they're here, and in fact we've already seen one, haven't we, Mr Gopal?"

Mr Gopal nodded energetically. "Yes. We saw a terribly big one only this morning. It was drinking from the river and I got a very good shot of it with my camera. I wish I could show you the picture, but it's not been developed yet."

The men stopped laughing. Billy noticed that one or two of them exchanged rather nervous glances.

"And what else have you heard about these tigers?" said their leader, mockingly. "Have you heard that they ride bicycles and eat bananas?"

Billy smiled. "No," he said. "Nobody has said anything about that. But we have been told that they're man-eaters."

As he spoke everybody became quite silent. The leader of the loggers stared at Billy, and Billy could see that there were tiny little drops of sweat forming on his forehead, just below his red handkerchief.

"Did you say man-eaters?"

"Yes," said Billy. "We heard that they ate ten men further down the river. It was terrible. Only their hats were left."

The loggers looked at one another again, and Billy decided it was time to go.

"Well," he said. "We mustn't keep you from your work. You've still got lots of those trees to cut down."

"Yes, indeed," said Mr Gopal as they turned to leave. "We shall just be on our way. And if you see these tigers, could you possibly let us know? I can't wait to photograph them again!"

Billy and Mr Gopal walked back down the path, leaving the men standing around the felled tree.

"It worked," whispered Billy to Mr Gopal. "It worked perfectly!"

Mr Gopal tried hard, but he could not help laughing.

"Oh, their faces!" he said. "Did you see how they looked at one another for support? Those men are scared absolutely stiff!"

"Yes," said Billy. "Now on to part two of the plan!"

~ 7 ~
Billy's Plan: Part Two

Back at Mr Bhalla's tree house, Billy recounted what had happened.

"It worked perfectly," he said. "But now we must get ready for the next stage of the plan. Mr Bhalla, have you got them?"

Mr Bhalla nodded. "I've laid them all out in the room next door," he said. "And Aunt Gopal has been busy doing some stitching."

"Good," said Billy. "That will be one for me, one for you, one for Mr Gopal, and one for Nicola."

Mr Bhalla opened the door with a flourish, and there in the next room, laid out on the floor before them, were four large tiger skins. Some of them had been used as rugs, and had holes here and there, but Mr Gopal's aunt had done her best with needle and thread and these holes now looked far better.

Billy was delighted. "I'll try mine first," he said. "Then you can all see what it looks like."

He dropped to his hands and knees, and Mr Gopal draped the skin over him, tying it underneath with strings which his aunt had cunningly sewn on. It was a perfect fit.

"Oh, my goodness!" exclaimed Mr Gopal. "A tiger! A tiger in this very room!"

Billy moved about a little, and gave a roar, just for effect.

"Oh!" shouted Mr Gopal. "My good-ness me! Please help us, please! A tiger!"

Nicola tried her skin next, and she, too, looked very realistic. Then it was the turn of Mr Gopal and Mr Bhalla, both of whom made very fine tigers indeed.

"This is wonderful," said Billy, from within his tiger skin. "Now let's take them off and get ready to go!"

They waited until it was late afternoon. India can get very hot, and nobody fancied spending much time in those heavy skins until it became a bit cooler. It was also better to wait, Billy thought, until it was getting just a little bit dark. Tigers look more frightening then.

After enjoying a final glass of the pink sherbet drink on the veranda, they bundled the tiger skins into one large bundle and Mr Bhalla lowered it to the ground on a rope. Then they all climbed down the ladders to the ground and set off along the path to the jungle. Mr Gopal's aunt had been invited to go with them, but, her work on the tiger skins over, she had chosen to stay with her new friends in the village.

"We must be very quiet," said Mr Bhalla. "Those men have sharp hearing."

They walked on, each person carrying a tiger skin under his arm. Each had his own thoughts. Billy thought: *I do hope this works. But what if they see the strings? What will they do to us?*

Mr Bhalla, for his part, thought: *If this fails, then they'll probably cut down the bubblegum trees even more quickly — just out of spite.*

Mr Gopal thought: *My goodness! Should I really be prowling around the jungles of India dressed in a tiger skin — at my age? Should I?*

And Nicola was just about to think: *Will the tail of my tiger skin . . .* when she stopped, and every thought left her mind. For there, directly in front of her on the path, was a large snake, coiled up and hissing, poised to strike!

Nicola stood stock still. She opened her mouth to shout out, but no sound came. She was utterly paralysed with fright.

"Nicola," called out Billy. "Don't hold us up! Come on!"

"Help!" squeaked Nicola at last, just managing to sound the word. "A snake!"

The other three stopped, and looked behind them.

"Oh no," muttered Mr Gopal. "A cobra! Oh, goodness!"

When Mr Bhalla saw what was happening, he stopped where he was, a short distance behind Nicola.

"Don't move," he whispered. "Stay absolutely still. If you move a muscle, that snake will strike. Understand?"

Nicola gave a groan. The snake was hardly more than a pace away from her, and it was clearly very angry indeed. It was her worst nightmare – her very worst nightmare – come true.

What took place next happened so quickly that Billy hardly saw what was going on. He noticed Mr Bhalla reach into his pocket and get something out, and then, with a flick of his wrist, toss it over Nicola's shoulder. That's madness, Billy thought. The snake will strike.

The snake did strike. With a sudden lightning movement it struck, but not at Nicola. The snake struck at the small square of bubblegum which Mr Bhalla had tossed towards it. And of course, with its snake's sharp eyesight, it caught the bubblegum effortlessly. Its jaws snapped shut, the fangs sinking into the soft pink gum.

Of course the snake was now quite helpless!

"Hssss," it went, from between its stuck-together jaws. "Hssss."

"It's completely harmless now," said Mr Bhalla, with a laugh. "You can even step right over it if you wish, Nicola. It will take hours, maybe even days, before it gets that gum out of its mouth!"

They left the angry, but now harmless, cobra behind them and continued on the path. They could see the bubblegum trees in the distance now and soon it would be time to get into the skins. Then the real excitement would start.

In the logging camp, the men had just finished work. They had had a hard day of cutting down bubblegum trees, and they were resting, while their cook prepared their evening meal. This was the time of the day that they always liked — when work was finished and they could sit about and chat outside their tents. But today there was something wrong.

"Do you think that business about tigers was true?" said one of the men. "I thought it was quite safe round here."

The other scratched his head. "I don't know. Why would that man lie to us? He seemed pretty sure that he had seen something. I think there might be tigers after all."

"If I see a tiger round here, I'm packing up and going," said another man. "I don't fancy being a tiger's breakfast."

"Neither do I," agreed another. "My wife doesn't want me to be eaten. She told me so herself."

The head man got to his feet. "Stop all this talk about tigers! I've told you before and I'll tell you again. This jungle is perfectly safe. There are no tigers."

Just then, from some thick growth behind one of the tents, there came a noise. It was not a loud noise, but it made every head in the camp turn and stare.

"What was that?" asked one man. "Did you hear it? There's something in those bushes over there."

"I heard something!" shouted another, rising to his feet and huddling up with one of his friends. "Do you think it could be . . . a . . . a . . . tiger?"

"Nonsense!" snapped the head man. "How many times do I have to tell you? THERE ARE NO TIGERS!"

He had barely finished speaking when another noise came from the bushes. This time it was unmistakable. It was a growl!

~ 8 ~
Tiger! Tiger!

From within the bushes, covered in his heavy tiger skin, Billy could just make out what was happening in the camp.

"They're getting nervous," he whispered to Mr Bhalla. "I think they heard your growl."

"Good," said Mr Bhalla. "Let's just wait a few minutes. Let them think about it for a while."

The men did think about it, and were clearly becoming more and more frightened. Several of them went to stand by the cooking fire, knowing that tigers were meant to be afraid of fire. Others stood close to the mouth of their tent, ready to dash inside if any tigers should appear.

"I think the time has come," said Billy quietly. "I'll go first."

On all fours, looking quite like a fierce tiger, Billy started to move slowly out of the bushes. As he did so, he turned his tiger head from side to side, as if he were sniffing at the evening air. Then, for good measure, he growled.

When the men in the camp saw him, a great shouting broke out.

"Look!" cried one. "Tiger! Tiger!"

"Where? Where?" shouted another.

"Over there, by the bushes! A tiger!"

As the shouting continued, Billy darted to another clump of bushes and disappeared.

"Calm down!" shouted the head man, who had been looking away when Billy appeared. "You're imagining things. I tell you again, THERE ARE NO TIGERS!"

"But there was one right there," howled one of the men. "A great big one!"

As they argued amongst themselves, Mr Gopal crawled out of the bushes and stretched out a great tiger claw.

"Oh!" shouted one of the men. "Another one! Oh, save us! Save us!"

"Where?" shouted the head man. "Where is it?"

He turned round, and saw Mr Gopal crawling across the ground to join Billy, closely followed by Mr Bhalla and Nicola.

"Hundreds of them!" shouted one of the men. "We're surrounded by tigers!"

This was the signal for all the men to start running around at once. Stumbling over one another, they rushed about, picking up their possessions. Then, their belongings in their arms, their axes and saws left behind on the ground, the men ran as fast as they could down to the river, where their boat was moored.

"Grrr!" roared Mr Bhalla. "Grrr! Grrr!"

The sound of the roaring made the men run even faster. And when they reached the river edge, they did not even climb into the boat, but leapt, like frightened rats.

In the bushes, the four tigers sat down and laughed more heartily than they had ever laughed before. Mr Gopal laughed so much that he almost choked, and he had to take his tiger head off to wipe the tears of mirth away from his eyes.

"I've never seen anybody look so frightened," he said. "They were terrified!"

"They won't be coming back here," said Mr Bhalla, a broad smile on his face. "That's the last we'll see of them."

"And your bubblegum trees are saved," said Billy. "That's the important thing."

*

They could have gone home right then, but Mr Bhalla thought that it would be a good idea to stay just a little longer, just in case the men looked back from the river. So they all refastened their tiger skins and got down on their hands and knees again. Then they walked out of the bushes, with the proud walk of a group of tigers who had just done a very good job.

They prowled around the abandoned camp, sniffing at the axes and giving the occasional roar. It was all going very well. It had been a wonderful plan, and nothing had gone wrong. Or at least, nothing had gone wrong until then. Then it happened.

"That was a good growl you made," said Mr Bhalla to Billy. "It sounded very fierce."

"But I didn't growl," said Billy. "Maybe it was Nicola."

"It wasn't me," muttered Nicola from within her tiger skin.

"Nor me," said Mr Gopal. "I didn't growl."

They all stopped. Who had growled? Had Mr Bhalla imagined it?

He had not. For now there came another growl, and this time it was even louder. Billy spun round, and looked behind him. There, on the edge of the camp, was a great tiger, sniffing at the air with its fine, proud tiger's nose. And this tiger, for a change, was real!

"Let's go!" cried Mr Bhalla. "If we scamper away he'll think we were just a passing band of tigers. Perhaps he'll pay no attention."

They started to run on all fours, as fast as they could. It was hard work, but they were managing quite well until Mr Gopal stumbled.

When the real tiger saw one of the other tigers fall, he pounced. He did not like the sight of these four rather peculiar-looking tigers, and he thought that he would teach this one a lesson.

The other three stopped and watched in horror as the great tiger landed on Mr Gopal's back and dug its claws into his tiger skin. Mr Gopal collapsed under the weight of the real tiger and closed his eyes. At any moment his tiger skin would come off, he thought, and the real tiger would find a tasty snack inside. What would it be like to be eaten by a tiger? Would it hurt, or would it all be over very quickly? *What will I taste like?* he thought miserably.

"Fight back, Mr Gopal!" shouted Billy. "Remember you're a Gopal!"

Inside the tiger skin, Mr Gopal heard Billy's voice and the words stirred him.

Remember you're a Gopal! Yes! He was a Gopal! He was the grandson of Sikrit Pal Praviwallah Gopal, after all, the man who had fought off a tiger by biting its tail!

Yes! That was it! Without wasting any more time, Mr Gopal reached out and grabbed the angry tiger by its tail. Then, opening his mouth as wide as he could, he popped the end of the tail inside and bit.

It did not taste very pleasant, and there was a great deal of fur. But Mr Gopal's teeth sank well into the tiger's tail and it gave a roar of pain.

"Take that!" muttered Mr Gopal from between his clamped teeth. "That'll teach you to jump on a Gopal!"

The bite was too much for the tiger. Releasing Mr Gopal from his grip, he turned round to lick gingerly at his sore tail. This gave Billy his chance. Rushing forward, he helped Mr Gopal to his feet and bundled him off down the path, followed by the other two, all running as fast as they possibly could. Everybody was back on two legs by now, and had turned into people again – very frightened people running down a path with a tiger not too far behind them.

"Will he follow us?" gasped Nicola. "I'm sure he'll be twice as angry now!"

"I'm afraid he might," panted Mr Bhalla. "Tigers get very cross about this sort of thing. They're not ones to give up easily. We shall have to climb a tree."

On hearing Mr Bhalla's suggestion, they all stopped and looked about them. The path on either side of them was flanked by great towering trees, and if they managed to scale one of these then the tiger might walk right past them.

"What about this one?" said Billy, pointing to a particularly tall tree. "There are enough low branches to give us a start."

"A splendid idea," said Mr Bhalla. "You children go first and Mr Gopal and I will follow."

It was not a difficult tree to climb, and soon all four of them were perched right up at the top, looking down through the leaves to the path far below. Now all they had to do was wait until the tiger went past. It would soon realise it had lost them, and all they would have to do then would be to wait a little while before they climbed down and made their way home.

The minutes went past slowly and Billy was beginning to wonder whether the tiger had gone in the other direction. Then suddenly Mr Bhalla touched Billy on the arm and pointed downwards.

"Tiger," he whispered. "Right below us."

Billy looked down. There on the path below them was the beautiful, sinewy figure of the tiger, padding slowly along, its nose raised to sniff the breeze for the scent of its enemies.

"Oh dear," said Mr Gopal. "It looks very cross."

"Well, it's not going to find us," said Billy quietly. "So you don't have to —"

He was about to say "worry", but before he had time to do so a terrible thing happened. Mr Gopal had taken a handkerchief out of his pocket to mop his brow and had unfortunately dropped it. Down through the leaves drifted the large white square of cloth, right down to the path, to land exactly in front of the great, angry tiger.

Of course the tiger looked up in surprise and saw, directly above it, four frightened human beings sitting on a very high branch. At the sight of this, it let out a great growl, which seemed to fill the forest with sound before it died away.

"Oh my goodness!" wailed Mr Gopal. "We are going to be entirely eaten up. This terrible beast will shin up our tree and eat us up – one, two, three, four. Every one of us."

But Mr Gopal was wrong. The tiger looked at the trunk of the tree, stretched its claws in and out, and then yawned.

"He's too lazy," said Mr Bhalla. "That's a typical tiger for you! He knows that he doesn't even have to try to climb the tree. All he has to do is lie there until we come down."

The tiger looked up again, gave another growl, and then lay down at the foot of the tree. There was no need for him to waste his energy – his lunch was up the tree, hanging on to a branch, but sooner or later it would have to come down, and by then he hoped he would have an even sharper appetite!

~ 9 ~
Bubblegum to the Rescue

They sat on their high branches, looking down at the patient tiger and wondering how long it would be before one of them was overcome by sleep and fell off. It could be a day or two, if they were lucky, or it could be before that.

Whenever it would be, it was not a nice thought.

Then, after about an hour, Mr Bhalla suddenly let out a cry.

"I've had a wonderful idea," he said. "Why didn't I think of it before?"

"What is it?" asked Mr Gopal. "Could it possibly help us?"

"Yes," said Mr Bhalla. "Do you know what sort of tree this is?"

"A bubblegum tree," said Billy. "Or at least it looks like one."

"Precisely," said Mr Bhalla. "And it's a very nice juicy one at that. If I cut a little hole here, sap will come out by the bucketful."

"But what use would that be?" asked Nicola. "It won't do us any good to sit up here and chew bubblegum!"

Mr Bhalla laughed. "Indeed it would not," he agreed. "What I propose is that we make a bungee rope out of the gum and then one of us can bounce down, give that tiger a bit of a fright, and then bounce back!"

Everybody was silent. It was a most peculiar plan, but then the Bubblegummies were most peculiar people.

Then Billy broke the silence. "But who will jump?" he asked.

Mr Bhalla smiled. "I was thinking you might like to do it, Billy," he said with a smile. "I hear that you were bungee jumping last night in the village, and you did it very well."

Billy swallowed hard. He really had no choice. They had to do something about the tiger and he might as well be the one to do it. But a bungee jump on to a tiger's back? That sounded even worse than biting a tiger's tail!

Mr Bhalla made a hole in the bark of the bubblegum tree and had soon extracted a large lump of soft pink sap in his cupped hands. He passed this to Nicola, showing her how to twist it into a rope. Then he made another hole and collected more sap and passed that on to Billy. Soon everybody had twisted a long piece of gummy rope, which Mr Bhalla tied together to make one long bungee jumping rope.

"Now," he said, tying one end of the rope to their branch. "Let's attach the other end round you, Billy, and then you'll be ready."

"But what do I do once I get down there?" asked Billy, his voice unsteady with fear.

"Pull its whiskers," said Mr Bhalla. "That's one thing which a tiger can't stand. If you pull its whiskers it will go away soon enough."

Billy looked down through the leaves to the waiting tiger. He closed his eyes and counted. One, two, three . . . now! Taking a deep breath, he cast himself off the branch, shooting down through the leaves, straight towards the tiger. Then, with a sudden lurch, he felt the bubblegum rope tighten and slow down his fall.

Mr Bhalla had calculated the length of the rope to perfection. Billy found himself just above the rather astonished tiger, and he was able to reach out and give the tiger's whiskers a good tweak. The tiger roared out in fury and slashed at Billy with his great claws, but he was too late – the bubblegum rope had yanked Billy up again

and the next thing the tiger saw was the boy disappearing through the leaves!

Down went Billy for the second time, and again he was able to give the tiger's whiskers a good pull before he shot up into the leaves. The tiger was even more furious this time, and by the time it had happened for a third time, the animal's patience was exhausted. With a great roar of disgust, it turned on its tail and shot off down the path, to vanish in the undergrowth.

"He's had enough," shouted Mr Bhalla triumphantly. "I knew he wouldn't like that! I knew it!"

They waited a few minutes to make sure that the tiger did not come back.

Then, once they were sure it was safe to do so, they climbed back down the tree and began the journey back to the village.

"I feel rather sorry for that poor tiger," said Billy to Mr Bhalla as they walked home. "I'm sure we made him feel rather miserable."

"Yes," said Mr Bhalla. "But you must remember that we also did him a big favour. By saving the forest, we've preserved a home for him. If the loggers had cut down all the trees, he would have had nowhere to go."

"So even if he is rather cross with us, we've still saved his life," said Billy.

"Exactly," said Mr Bhalla. "Just so."

*

When everybody in the village heard about what had happened, they were overjoyed.

"Our trees are saved!" they cried. "And we owe it all to your plan, Billy."

Billy, of course, was very modest. "I was only one of the tigers," he said. "Everybody was brave."

They were too tired to celebrate that night, and decided that they would have a village party the next day. So they all went to bed in their rooms high up in Mr Bhalla's tree house, and they all, in their different ways, dreamed about what had happened that day. In Billy's dream he was prowling around in a tiger skin, growling through his teeth. In Nicola's dream there was a snake blowing bubbles through its tightly-clamped jaws. Mr Bhalla dreamed of bubblegum trees, safe again. And Mr Gopal – well, he dreamed that he was biting a tiger's tail while his grandfather, Sikrit Pal Praviwallah Gopal, looked on with pride.

The next morning, the entire village was up early, getting ready for the party. Great dishes of food were prepared in the high tree-kitchens, sending delicious odours wafting through the branches. The school was closed for the day – to mark the occasion – and everybody was in a festive mood.

Mr Bhalla was particularly excited. He dressed in his finest outfit – a gold and white tunic which had belonged to his father, who had been an official elephant driver, a mahout, to the Maharajah of Chandipore. Billy, who had not brought any special clothes with him, was lent a party tunic by one of the Bubblegummie boys, and Nicola was given a green and gold sari to wear. Everybody looked very smart indeed.

The party began with a feast. This was a magnificent affair, with all sorts of delicious foods set out on broad green leaves freshly picked from banana trees. There were curries and pickles and large dishes of dried coconut. There were poppadoms stacked one hundred high, and great mounds of bananas fried in sugared yoghurt!

But most delicious of all was a dish which had been made by Mr Gopal's aunt. She had not wasted her time while the others were away being chased by tigers. She had been learning recipes from her new friends and, with a little help, she had cooked the most wonderful bubblegum pudding anybody had ever tasted. It was an extraordinary dish - a pudding you could chew on for as long as you liked and then blow into great big bubbles before you swallowed. The

Bubblegummie children were used to this sort of thing, of course, but for Billy and Nicola it was quite unlike anything they had ever eaten before, and twice as nice.

After the feast there were competitions, including a most exciting game of tree hide-and-seek. This was far more thrilling – and dangerous – than an ordinary game of hide-and-seek, as you had to hide in the branches, which was not always easy. There was also a bungee jumping competition – which Nicola won – and, finally, a bubblegum-blowing contest. Billy entered this, and did quite well, but not as well as Mr Gopal himself, who blew a bubble so large that even the Bubblegummies were impressed.

"We are so very grateful to you," said Mr Bhalla, as the party came to an end. "It would have been a tragedy if those men had destroyed our bubblegum trees. Now, thanks to you, the trees will survive. And of course we shall be able to send Mr Gopal his supplies again."

"It was no trouble at all," said Billy. "I'm glad to have helped."

He knew, of course, that it could all have turned out quite differently. The snake could have bitten Nicola. The men could have guessed that the tigers weren't real. The real tiger could have eaten Mr Bhalla.

But none of these things had happened, and so there was no point in worrying about it.

They left the following morning. Mr Bhalla helped them into the flying boat, and then he and just about everybody from the village stood at the edge of the river and waved as the ancient plane taxied out to start its take-off.

"Goodbye!" shouted Mr Bhalla, as the plane began to skim over the water. "Come back and see us soon!"

"We shall!" cried Billy, waving from his window.

Then the plane was in the air, and the river and the jungle fell away beneath them. They had a long flight ahead of them, but Mr Bhalla had given them plenty of bubblegum for the trip. So that would keep them busy enough.

As the plane gained height, Billy craned his neck to get a last glimpse of the ground below them. There was the village, with its walkways and swinging bridges; there was Mr Bhalla's house in its tall tree. And there, of course, were the bubblegum trees themselves, towering higher than all the other trees, and safe now – Billy hoped – for at least another hundred years.

Ladies and gentlemen, boys and girls,
step right up for an amazing circus story
by Alexander McCall Smith . . .

Freddie Mole,
Lion Tamer

Freddie Mole is an ordinary boy who gets a
cleaning job at the circus. He can't believe his luck
when he is asked to understudy some of the acts.
But can he really tame four growling lions?

Coming Spring 2016

Join Akimbo and the wild animals on the game
reserve for a wonderful African adventure . . .

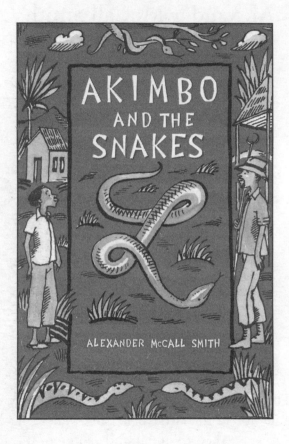

Akimbo loves learning about all the snakes in Uncle
Peter's snake park. But things get even more exciting
when a green mamba is spotted in the wild, and Akimbo
and his uncle set off on a dangerous mission to catch it!

Return to the game reserve for another wild adventure with Akimbo . . .

A lady comes to study the baboons in the game reserve where Akimbo's father is head ranger. Akimbo and his cousin are keen to help. But life out in the bush isn't easy – for Akimbo or the baboons! Perhaps they can learn from each other . . .